Winning C

A Bachelor Brothers of S

Mel Teshco

Winning Offer
Copyright © 2024 Mel Teshco

Cover Art by Emcat Designs
https://www.facebook.com/EmCatDesigns

Chapter One

Harper Franks twirled the pink paper parasol inside her now empty glass as Liam Black flirted with her near the dance floor of the Black Pearl Nightclub. Damn, he was sexy. Blond hunks weren't her usual type, but this man was sculptured perfection. That he towered over everyone else in the club and made her feel small in stature only increased her awareness of him.

Her lashes fluttered closed. She'd bet he'd be able to hold her one-handed against the wall while he fucked her and used his other hand to play with her body. Heat surged between her thighs and she resisted moaning at the images filling her head.

Shit. She needed to stop thinking about him in that way.

Her sole purpose for being here was to check out the auction from afar and ascertain if the men who bid on the women really were wealthy beyond compare. Not that she'd been able to go into the actual function room where the auction was being held, but it'd been enough for her to discreetly watch the men from afar as they'd arrived for the event.

They'd exuded wealth as they'd rocked up in their sports cars and designer suits, flashing their gold watches and polished shoes while showing off their perfect hairstyles and gleaming white teeth along with their auras of invulnerability. It wasn't until her stare at latched onto a sheikh—they were notoriously generous—and she'd done a quick google search of him to discover he was filthy rich, that she comprehended this was a very real opportunity.

Then she overheard a female staff member bragging that the sheikh had come to every auction since its conception, and she knew for sure he was the man she'd try to wow at the next auction.

In the meantime she'd keep renovating her crumbling country home with its eight bedrooms and thirty-five acre parcel of land. That it was heavily mortgaged was the only reason she was here now figuring out her future.

She intended to agist horses on the land whilst renovating what would become her dream bed and breakfast, but she needed finances to do that and, in the present economy, no bank would even look at her.

She pushed her shoulders back, determination filling her from the inside out. The auction would change all that. She'd do whatever was needed to live the dream she and her father had shared.

That her favorite charity would also benefit was just an added incentive.

Her father would be proud of her initiative.

But first she had to convince whoever bid on her to invest in her property. Preferably the sheikh. She'd need to study what Sheikh Korian liked in his women so she knew how to dress and act accordingly.

She'd bait the hook, she only hoped he'd reel her in.

The club's loud techno music muted in her mind as she sank deeper into introspection, dreaming of her future. She'd fix the land first, clear away all the lantana and other weeds, then divide the acreage into small paddocks with railed fencing and basic shelters for horses. That the property was less than an hour to Sydney, where land was scarce, meant she'd make a decent income from agistment alone.

"Earth to Harper!"

She blinked and smiled at Liam who stood in front of her, his beer in one hand and a drink for her in his other.

He held up the frosty glass. "I thought you might be thirsty."

A frisson of awareness burned through her. A pity the sheikh she'd set her mind on didn't look like this Adonis. "Thank you, I am rather parched."

Liam bent, his hair brushing hers and his voice a caress near her ear. "I hope this isn't too forward, but from the moment I saw you all I wanted was to strip off your clothes and possess your body."

A hot shiver skated through her and she almost groaned aloud at his honesty. She'd never appreciated people who danced around the truth. She liked that Liam was confident and open, and didn't pretend commitment was a part of his future plans.

But he needed to learn he couldn't always be the one in control.

She hadn't yet accepted her drink, and with his hands full and his ability to touch her now impossible, she lifted her arm up and over his shoulder, snaking it behind his neck. "You should be so lucky," she said softly, cupping the bulge of his erection with her other hand.

His breath hissed simultaneously with hers. Heavens above, he was frigging huge, his cock matching the rest of him. Wetness slicked her thighs and his nostrils flared, as though he scented her arousal.

She released him with a blink of shock, taking her proffered drink with a shaky hand. She sucked on the straw, drinking down the vodka and pineapple juice mix. Heaven only knew she needed some kind of fortification.

He lifted his beer and gulped it down, his eyes gleaming.

The next thing she knew, he was getting rid of their empty drinks, then guiding her away from the bar and its crowd of people, and into a corner of the room where a big, currently unused speaker hid them from view and blocked out much of the noise.

He pushed her against the wall, one of his hands supporting his weight on the wall above her head, the other hand cupping her face as his blue stare darkened like a savage thunderstorm. "Did you enjoying playing with fire?"

She arched a brow, the flash of Technicolor lights making him look as surreal as a phantom and twice as dangerous. She ignored the fleeting knowledge that it only made her wetter for him. "Probably about as much as you enjoyed stoking the flames," she said huskily.

His eyes flashed. "Why do I get the impression you're just too good to be true?" he muttered. "And that I should get away from you now before it's too late."

"And yet you're going to ignore your instincts and better judgment, aren't you?" she asked sweetly.

Electricity gathered in the air between them, a frisson of power jolting through her even before he growled low in his throat and said, "You really are perfect for me."

Keeping his hand in place, he dropped his head so that his mouth slammed over hers, dominating the kiss that might have been bruising if she wasn't kissing him back just as fiercely.

He was just the distraction she needed right now.

She was still fighting grief after the loss of her father a little under six months ago, add in the weight of their dream that now verged on a nightmare of creating a bed and breakfast, and she wanted this piece of heaven with Liam even more.

Their chemistry was explosive, her yearning to have him buried between her thighs while he exorcised the grief right out of her head now all too clear. She needed this...needed him.

He was still kissing her when he dropped his hand from her face and slid it under her short skirt. With deft ease, he pushed aside her thong and flicked her clit with his thumb.

She jerked and gasped, her wide eyes staring up into his. "People are watching us!"

His smile didn't seem to reach his eyes, not with his stare so sharply focused on her. "No one can see the bottom half of you," he said thickly. "The speaker conceals you from the side and my body conceals you from every other angle. You're safe."

"Is that what you say to all the girls you make out with at the club?"

"Only the ones who look like they need stimulation," he purred thickly.

Her heart stuttered. "And I look like I need that?"

He nodded, then said softly, "You do."

He massaged her nub a little harder and her head fell back as delicious currents of desire pulsed through her. Within seconds she was at the point where she didn't care if every eye was on them while she fell apart under his ministrations. In some ways, it turned her on even more. Let them look if that was what they wanted. All she wanted was to orgasm and be reminded that life wasn't all stress and hard work.

"Just how many other girls have you've been with who looked like they needed this...stimulation?" she asked in a croaky voice, electricity burning through her.

"Just you," he admitted. "I've never made another woman climax here in the nightclub."

She squirmed against his hand even as she blinked up at him. "Do you really mean that?"

"I don't make a habit of lying just to get into a woman's pants." He paused, as though waiting for her to disagree.

Her eyes narrowed. She'd been so close to orgasm! Had he deliberately stopped? "I'm not about to argue the point. Keep doing what you were doing."

His eyes burned like blue flames. "You're about to come hard, my gorgeous wildflower."

Her pussy clenched at his words, even as she asked, "*Wildflower*?"

He continued deftly massaging her with one hand while he used his other to reverently touch her hair. "Your strawberry blonde hair reminds me of a wildflower. Those ones with white petals and the faintest hue of pink."

She gasped, pleasure thrumming through her veins. "That's kind of cute."

"*Cute* wasn't exactly the word I was going for when you're about to come," he said hoarsely, before he slid a finger deep inside her.

She wanted to thrust against his hand for long, pleasurable hours, but at this rate she'd be lucky to last another minute. She needed this so badly. She sucked in a gasp as liquid heat drenched her thighs and his fingers, stars bursting behind her eyes even as she was thrown up to the heavens where other stars shone just as brightly.

Holy shit.

She'd never orgasmed this hard, and never from a stranger's touch. She'd had a handful of lovers, each one as progressively worse as the last. She realized now she'd been with duds. Liam's handiwork had quickly opened her eyes to that solid little fact.

He withdrew his hand and tucked her thong back into place, then lifting his hand, he sucked on the finger he'd pushed deep inside her. "You taste as good as you look, wildflower."

A shudder of need throbbed through her. She might have orgasmed, but the lioness inside her wanted more. She wanted him to fuck her completely, to fill her with his huge cock and make her come harder than she'd ever come before.

She exhaled and crossed her arms, adopting a standoffish position. "That was...nice, thank you."

He cocked a brow. "Nice?" His gaze brushed over her face, as though assessing her mental state. "Looks like I'll have to up my game if that's all I get from this delicious little interlude."

She pulled her skirt back into place, patting down any imaginary creases. "I'm sure you'll have women lined up waiting to tell you how perfect you are in bed." She stepped around him, all too aware she'd left her clutch bag beneath one of the tables next to the long bar. "If you'll excuse me, I—"

"This isn't over," he growled low and rumbly next to her ear, one of his hands holding her close. "This is just the beginning."

She shrugged free of his clasp, though it took everything she had not to wilt against his strength, his desire to prolong their intimacy. "I realize you wouldn't be used to girls saying *no* to you, but this really is goodbye."

She had to leave him before all her well-laid plans were diluted by some shallow sexual interlude. Her future depended on her being cautious and devoted to her cause.

She stepped away from him, being careful not to twist her ankle in the silly high heels she'd worn to blend in with the other women. She was more of a boots and jeans kind of girl, and was stifled in the city with all the trendy outfits that women seemed compelled to wear as though they were in a beauty competition.

At finding her clutch bag where she'd left it—thankfully it hadn't been stolen—she scooped it up, all too aware of how wobbly her legs were thanks to the orgasm Liam had gifted her. She actually owed him big time for the temporary reprieve of stress, and felt a touch guilty for not returning the favor.

That he'd probably have his pick of women wanting to suck him dry after she left shouldn't make her insides prickle with envy. Liam wasn't her type, and she'd bet she wasn't his type, either.

It wasn't until she'd skirted around the dance floor, with its heaving mass of bodies dancing to the techno rhythm, and was heading toward the front exit doors, that she found Liam waiting for her. The noise was easily half as intense where he stood, and she asked without shouting, "What are you doing here?"

"I'm waiting to escort you safely to your car."

An unwanted, thrilling charge poured through her. "I didn't realize you were a gentleman."

"That's because I'm still a stranger to you."

A stranger who'd taken the edge off her tension and made her feel alive for the first time in too long.

Her heels clacked across the pavement as they walked past security and the crowd of partygoers still lining up to enter the nightclub. The air was chilly outside, with remnants of rain staining the sidewalk and asphalt, neon lights reflected on the wet surfaces.

She nodded at her white SUV in the parking bay ahead. Her vehicle was way past its prime, but she'd put off buying a new one to instead put what money she had into fixing her country home and property. She stopped at the driver's side, trying not to shiver at how close Liam stood beside her.

It'd be so easy to ask for a repeat performance from him, before begging him to go the whole way. At least she'd have some pleasant memories to take with her.

She cleared her throat and her mind. "Well, thank you for walking me to my car. And for...the great night."

He brushed back a piece of her hair, then leaned down to kiss her with a tenderness that almost undone her. It was far easier for her to repel him when it was nothing but lust sizzling between them.

He pulled back, then conceded softly, "I don't want this to be goodbye."

She reached up and traced his mouth with her fingertip. He had gorgeous lips for a man, a mouth made for kissing. She would have loved to see what that same mouth might have done to other places on her body. She dropped her arm as though his lips had burned her, and yet it took everything she had to turn her back on him and open her door. "We don't always get what we want."

It took even more willpower not to take one last look at the man outside her window as she shut the door and fired up the engine. It wasn't until after she'd backed out of the parking bay, then cruised forward onto the road, that she looked in her rearview mirror.

Liam hadn't moved and stood next to the road staring after her, his face set with purpose and his blond hair glinting angelically under the streetlights.

Chapter Two

One year later...

Liam greeted the influential and esteemed men as they stepped inside the function room holding tonight's auction. A pair of bouncers stood just outside the double doors, where a large foyer separated the auction from the nightclub.

Security was necessary to ensure no uninvited guests tried to sneak inside and ogle the women who'd later come out on stage, with a mission to wow the affluent men who'd bid on them.

Liam smiled and nodded at the sheikh who was dressed in a cream Brioni suit and keffiyeh headwear. Korian was always the epitome of affluence. That he'd been a regular for the once-yearly auction event was quite the feather in the cap for the Black brothers. No doubt the sheikh would bid an outrageous amount on whichever woman caught his eye tonight like he had every other year.

Not that Liam had been too focused on last year's auction. He'd been a little preoccupied, absent from much of his duties thanks to the woman in the adjoining Black Pearl Nightclub who'd made him forget pretty much everything but her name.

Harper.

A pity he'd never learned her last name. She'd been a bright star in his world for just a few hours and then she'd gone and everything had faded back to gray with her absence.

He shook free his thoughts to focus back on his job. The room was nearly filled to capacity when the last of the clientele stepped into the room and grabbed a bidding paddle. Liam nodded at the young, well-dressed man before closing the doors behind him.

When he turned back, his brother Aiden, approached with a clipboard in hand. Liam nodded at him. "Still refusing to use technology I see."

Aiden glanced at the clipboard. "Some of the ladies prefer not to have their names recorded online, so I'm happy to oblige." He shrugged. "And it's not like we need to know anything more about them other than what they look like. Let's face it, it's all the men here care about."

Liam winced, but his brother was right. Beauty was what drew the men to these auctions, along with the adrenaline of the bid. And though the women had to give at least the barest of information about themselves prior to the auction, it was destroyed once the auction ended, along with the names on paper that were attached to Aiden's clipboard.

"Who have we got tonight?" Liam asked.

Aiden handed him the clipboard and attached list of names. "Take a look, though whether these women are using their real identity or not is up to them."

Liam glanced at the names in the order of their auction appearance. His eyes paused on the third name down. His throat drying, he glanced at his brother. "Harper Franks?"

Aiden nodded and smiled. "I don't doubt for a second Sheikh Korian will bid hard on her."

Liam's heart twisted. How ironic. After all, how many Harpers could there possibly be out there? Or was some higher force trying to fuck with his head?

"She's not just a looker, she's really sweet," Aiden added.

So had the Harper Liam had gotten to know. Not that she'd ever consider auctioning herself off. Despite the wild side he'd brought out of her, she'd seemed far too virtuous for that.

You might have slid a finger inside her and made her orgasm, but you knew nothing about her...including her last name.

"I only hope she's resilient enough to handle whoever bids on her," Aiden said mildly.

Liam handed back the clipboard. "I'm sure the sheikh will make her very happy," he said tonelessly. He'd heard the women Korian had bid on in the past had come away with either priceless jewelry or cash.

Aiden frowned, but before he could ask any questions, the auctioneer stepped onto the stage and greeted everyone with his usual spiel. "Gentlemen, I want to thank you all for attending tonight. I'm sure our ladies and their charities will appreciate your time and effort."

A smattering of polite applause went around the room, most of the men just eager to get the formalities out the way to begin the night's bidding.

"I hope you're all feeling generous," the auctioneer added. "If not, there is always your cold, hard bed to keep you company later tonight—not that I'm suggesting sex is a sure thing, *that* will be up to the discretion of the ladies tonight you bid on."

A few of the men laughed, though the sheikh looked uninspired as he stood with his arms crossed and a paddle dangling from one of his hands while he stared at the empty stage.

Liam nodded at the auctioneer, silently communicating to wrap up the pre-talk and get on with it.

The auctioneer nodded back, his gaze expansive as he took in the crowd of men in front of him. "But I'm sure you're all eager to begin the show—am I right?" An enthusiastic roar filled the room and he grinned and shouted, "Then let's get the first girl out here!" As the cheering died off, he added, "Meet Chelsea!"

A dark woman with frizzy hair and gorgeous plump lips highlighted in crimson stepped out onto the stage in a skin-tight leotard and skyscraper heels. The music played and she began to perform an athletic dance routine that had the men hooting even before she stripped to her barely-there underwear beneath.

This wasn't a strip show by any means, but the ladies were encouraged to either wear something skimpy to start with, or put on a show that might rouse extra bids.

Galan moved through the crowd to stand next to Liam before handing him a bidding paddle. "I have a good feeling you'll need this tonight, brother."

Liam shook his head. Thanks to these auctions, Galan had found the love of his life three years ago, Aiden then succumbing to one of the women on stage the following year. Last year Liam had missed out on the lucky streak. He didn't doubt this year would be the same.

He'd already met—and lost—the woman of his dreams.

The gavel banged, the auction won by a bald, unsmiling man in a too-tight suit. It wasn't until he helped his woman off the stage that his fleshy lips curled into a grin. It was clear he thought he'd be getting lucky tonight, though whether or not that eventuated would be up to the woman he'd bid on.

Liam turned to his older brother. "Not everyone is destined to find the love of their lives at this auction." He cocked a brow. "Or be a devoted dad to twins."

Galan's smile was soft. "I am a lucky bastard, aren't I?" He clapped a hand on Liam's shoulder. "But if Aiden and I can find happiness, then you most definitely can too." He winked. "I'm banking on it!"

Liam narrowed his eyes as Galan turned away with a chuckle, then disappeared into the crowd. That he was easily half-a-head taller than most of them meant he didn't easily disappear anywhere. But that wasn't what Liam was paying attention to.

Had Galan—*both* his brothers—put a wager on him bidding for a woman? That Liam had once bet Galan would bid on a woman seemed like a lifetime ago now. Of course, Liam had known Layla was one of the girls who'd been about to step onto stage, so his bet had been almost failsafe. It had been obvious to everyone but Galan that he was in love with Layla.

Galan had likely fallen in love with her from the moment he'd met her.

Just like Liam had fallen for Harper.

A red-haired woman sashed out on stage wearing a formal dress, except he wouldn't exactly call it formal when it bared more skin than fabric. The woman got the desired result though when the men raised paddles amongst wolf whistles and groans.

He glanced at Sheikh Korian. He looked...bored.

Shit.

If word got out that the infamous sheikh was losing interest, their once-yearly auction might very well suffer.

He nodded at one of the waitresses, Fiona, who was dressed in her skimpy lingerie while delivering drinks to the men on a tray. She glanced his way and he nodded meaningfully toward the sheikh. She nodded back, her long black hair swishing as she walked to Sheikh Korian, offering him a drink along with a flirtatious smile.

The sheikh took a flute of champagne with a returned smile, his gaze trawling over her barely-there outfit before he reached into his pocket and withdrew a handful of big notes. When he placed them on the tray, the remaining flutes wobbled as Fiona inhaled sharply, not expecting such a serious tip.

Liam's tension eased. The sheikh had just needed to find a woman to intrigue him. Thankfully, Korian was no longer bored. No doubt he'd focus on the waitress as much as the auction itself now.

The auctioneer's hammer went down for the second time, the man who'd won the lady *whooping* before he jogged up to the stage and drew his woman down into his arms.

The auctioneer grinned. "Another happy winner. Let's keep it going for the third lady up for bid. And seriously, who doesn't love a cowgirl? Let's make some noise for Harper!"

A country rock song started up even as a woman in a cowboy hat, a tiny white skirt, spiked knee-high boots and a pink V-neck tank with tassels hanging from the fabric stalked out like a goddess on stage, a whip dragging along behind her.

Liam couldn't breathe, not while his heart was lodged in his throat.

It really was Harper.

His Harper.

Chapter Three

Harper was aware of Liam even before she saw him in the crowd. If her mouth hadn't already been dry and her pulse sky-rocketing—they were now! He was still as gorgeous as ever, still commandeered a room. She swallowed hard. She had to stick to her plan. She had to show no inhibitions whatsoever.

She had to own the stage.

If she didn't she would most certainly lose everything. And she couldn't allow that. It didn't stop her peripheral vision from seeing Liam press his phone to his ear. A frown threatened. Who the hell could he be talking to in the middle of the auction?

Her auction?

She focused on Sheikh Korian. He was ogling her and the whip in her hand. Any hint of a frown dissolved as she secretly smiled. She'd uncovered rumors about his sexual preferences and his fondness for pain. She lifted the handle and struck the stage with a *crack*.

The sheikh licked his lips. *Oh, yes.* The whip was definitely doing the trick.

That Liam's eyes burned into her like a brand didn't mean anything, she *refused* to allow it to mean anything. Sheikh Korian might not satisfy her in bed like she was sure Liam would, but the sheikh *would* satisfy her desire to keep the estate she and her dad had had big dreams about.

Not only would she keep her property with its big and dilapidated home, she'd hopefully restore it to its original glory.

She swayed her hips as she unbuttoned her tasseled shirt, then wrenched it open as she stared at the sheikh in his suit and keffiyeh.

Her breasts all but spilled free, the skimpy lace bra barely restraining them.

Sheikh Korian raised his paddle, his hawkish nose prominent above his dark beard. "One hundred thousand dollars."

For a first bid it was almost obscene. Few would match it. She smiled demurely at him as she fondled the whip's handle. She had no idea how far she'd go with the Middle Eastern man, she had no idea if she'd even consider having sex with him. But it was somewhat of a general consensus that sex was part of the package, despite a contract saying consent had to be mutual.

The audience muttered and looked at one another. Few could afford to top that bid and she doubted anyone would. She twirled the whip around her like it was an extension to her body, giving a performance that would no doubt impress the sheikh who'd just earned her for the night.

She stopped the motion then slid the thong of the whip up her body and between her breasts even as she distantly heard the auctioneer counting down.

"Going once, going twice—"

"Two hundred and fifty thousand."

She froze at the commanding voice, and it took everything she had to move her head and eye the bidder who'd just offered a quarter of a million dollars for her. She did a slow blink, her heart thudding dully in ears before becoming a roar.

Liam. His bidding paddle was still in the air, his stare resolute.

She swallowed hard. She wanted to believe it possible that he'd been so captivated by her and their intense encounter a year ago that he wanted more. But she'd known the moment she'd left he would have found some other woman to cozy up with. His foreplay with her would have become nothing but a fleeting memory.

So why had he just bid a small fortune on her? The Black brothers were wealthy, but surely none of them were *that* wealthy?

She covered her mouth with a shaky hand, her shock turning to outrage. How was she going to save her property now? She'd banked on the sheikh either investing in her future bed and breakfast horse property, or possibly giving her an amazing tip that he was renowned for.

No doubt Liam had spent his savings now on getting the one woman who'd slipped through his fingers.

The auctioneer's gavel cracked decisively against its sound block. "Sold! To our very own Liam Black." He cleared his throat and added, "And number sixty-nine, no less."

A few men chuckled, but Harper barely registered their mirth. Not when everything inside her screamed with injustice. He wasn't in love with her—he couldn't possibly be in such a short time—he wanted to finish what they'd started, and nobody, not even a super-rich sheikh, was going to stop him.

Her legs were suddenly too weak to move her across the stage to where Liam waited. It didn't stop him. He jumped up onto the platform and stalked toward her, then picked her up so that she had no choice but to link her ankles behind him and cling on as he bent her back and kissed her senseless.

Her hat fell onto the floor, her hair spilling free as their avid audience whooped and cheered at the spectacle. She'd never been an exhibitionist but the other men faded into the background as she had an out-of-body experience that had to be from shock. Too bad her senses latched onto the man who'd filled her dreams and fantasies too many times to count.

She shouldn't want this...shouldn't want *him*.

She'd counted on a meaningless and no strings attached night with the sheikh. It would have been easy then to walk away from him in the morning with a heavy purse and her future secured.

That her body still reacted to Liam so strongly, her pulse fluttering along with her nerve endings that had come back to life wherever he touched left her reeling. It'd taken her a whole year to try and forget this man. How long would it take her after spending the night with him?

Liam groaned before he dragged his lips from hers, his eyes though watching her as though she was a butterfly under a microscope. "We meet again, wildflower," he said thickly.

She nodded, her throat too scratchy for conversation and her emotions reeling.

He tightened his hold on her. "I've been waiting for you to return."

He had? Surely he had plenty of other women lined up to be with him? He was a famous Black brother. They were notorious womanizers, and little wonder. They had looks, charisma and wealth. No doubt Liam need only to click his fingers and women came running.

Perhaps that was the appeal. She hadn't run to him, she'd run *from* him.

His eyes burned. "And this time we're finishing what we started."

Chapter Four

Liam watched Harper closely, noting how her dark golden-brown eyes flashed and her muscles tensed, as though fighting this intense attraction they shared.

"You have one night with me," she reminded.

"A lot can happen in one night," he said silkily.

He'd make sure of it.

But first...

He glanced back. The sheikh looked pissed. *Too bad*. The man could have easily thrown a million dollars away and not made a dent in his bank account. It was more about pride than finances when it came to Sheikh Korian.

Liam nodded at Fiona once again and she smiled and headed toward the sheikh with more drinks, her pushed-up breasts jiggling. No doubt she'd tucked away her good-sized tip already and would be on the hunt for more. Hopefully she'd keep Korian occupied for a good while. The last thing Liam needed was for the man to be offended or aggrieved by his losing bid.

Liam didn't search the crowd for his brothers. He wasn't sure whether they'd be pleased or peeved with his choice knowing the sheikh had bid on her first. In that moment he didn't particularly care. They'd gotten their women...it was his turn.

Pivoting with his prize still in his arms, Liam stalked to the back of the stage and through the curtains. A couple of half-dressed women squealed and covered themselves as he stalked past them.

"Where are you taking me?" Harper squeaked.

"To the lockers so you can change back into whatever you wore here," he said, putting her down in front of a row of them so she could open her locker door.

She pulled out jeans and a button-up white blouse. She looked down at her feet. "These boots are my every day wear," she said with a shy laugh, one that was the antithesis to the bold woman on stage.

He nodded, waiting until after she was dressed, with her stage outfit placed into the locker along with her bag before he took her hand and brought her with him down the steps at the back of the stage. Ignoring the side door leading to the nightclub, he strode back into the function room and past the male bidders, many of whom whistled and applauded at seeing them leaving together.

Aiden and Galan stood next to the sheikh, listening intently to whatever their biggest client was saying, when they all looked toward Liam. Though his brothers smiled and nodded, Korian's eyes flashed darkly.

Liam ignored them all to exit the building with Harper. Once outside, he led her to a silver, low slung sports car he'd left parked down the street, opening the passenger door for her.

She paused, her brow creasing. "Where are we going?"

He lifted his hand, tracing the stubborn set of her jaw as he said softly, "If we only have tonight, I want to experience all the things with you."

"As in first date kind of things?" she asked with rounded eyes.

Clearly she'd imagined he'd be taking her straight to bed, if she allowed it, to get his money's worth from her and take her in every sexual position imaginable. His dick thickened, reminding him that *was* part of his plans, just...not yet.

He wanted to romance her first and foremost, get into her head and find out about her in the short time he had before he got to know her physically.

He nodded. "Spot on, wildflower." He gestured for her to get into the car. "After you."

She giggled and saluted, "Yes, sir," before she did as he asked.

He somehow ignored the jolt of lust pouring through him as her shirt rode up and her denim pulled tight across her slender thighs before he shut her door and stalked around to the driver's seat.

He pulled out onto the road, glancing at the woman next to him. With her loose, strawberry blonde hair fluttering in the breeze and her taut body already relaxing a little, her lips curled into a smile while her golden-brown eyes warmed, he was glad he'd ignored his primal urge to take her to bed and had instead decided to take her out.

But the intermittent flashes of streetlights couldn't hide the sometimes pensive look on her face. She wasn't as brave as she pretended. He slowed for a red light. What had brought her back here? Yes, many men gave very generous tips to the women they bid on, but there was no guarantee.

Was that why she'd been focused on the sheikh? He was renowned for his outrageous tipping.

Liam flicked on his indicator and parked on the side of the road next to a small Mexican restaurant that, despite the late hour, was full of diners. He turned to Harper. "Are you hungry?"

She nodded. "Starving."

"Then I hope you enjoy Mexican food."

"Are you kidding? I love it."

She sounded shocked that he imagined otherwise, like he knew every facet of her life, her likes and dislikes. That he knew so little about her irked him no end, but tonight he planned to change that.

They were soon seated at a private little table with a red and white checkered tablecloth, where a cactus-shaped candle flickered gaily between them. The look was corny but endearing, as were the cactus lanterns glowing along the walls and the sombrero hats hanging from the ceiling.

He ordered margaritas and burritos, their drinks coming out first. It was a pleasure just to watch Harper take a sip and close her eyes as though she was in heaven. Or perhaps she was thankful for the Dutch courage the drink would give her. He'd bid so high on her she probably imagined he'd have even higher expectations in the bedroom.

He would have bid a lot more if necessary. For a guy who routinely forgot a woman the moment she left his bed, that he hadn't been able to get Harper out of his head from the moment he'd met her was something he needed to investigate a whole lot closer.

He leaned back in his chair. "So tell me about yourself? What made you enter the auction?"

She shrugged. "Like most everyone else there, I needed the money. And since it doesn't grow on trees...here I am." She bit her bottom lip. "The fact it helped my favorite charity made it a win-win for me."

She had to realize income wasn't a part of the bid, only her chosen charity received anything—unless the man she ended up with gave her a bonus afterward. He frowned. *Shit*. Had he been right in thinking she'd actually hoped the sheikh might win her, hence the shaky hand she'd pressed to her mouth when Liam had won her instead?

At the time he'd believed it'd been the hefty amount he'd bid, but maybe she'd been genuinely upset he'd won and Korian had lost?

Sheikh Korian really was beyond generous. If he'd given Fiona an amazing tip just for a drink and a smile, Liam could only imagine what a whole night with the man might bequeath. Ignoring his tightening chest, he asked, "What charity?"

"Horse Rescue Australia."

He raised a brow. "So the cowgirl costume wasn't just fantasy, you really are a horse girl?"

"Yes, I guess I am."

The burritos came out then, and she waited for the young waiter to leave before she shrugged and said, "I've spent half my life around horses. What I wore on stage made me feel more comfortable than what I would have in a bikini or underwear." She held his stare. "Enough about me though, it's your turn."

She bit into her burrito while he began a spiel about himself, or at least, the business side of things. After all, it was becoming pretty clear that was all she cared about. She wasn't here hoping for a future relationship with someone affluent, she just wanted a piece of their wealth.

"Most of my work centers on the Black Pearl Nightclub and function rooms, along with the Garden Café restaurant. But I've also recently invested in a handful of other businesses that have paid me dividends."

She swallowed, her eyes going wide. "So you really could part with a quarter-million without getting heartburn over it?"

He picked up his burrito, caution now flooding through him. He'd imagined she wasn't corrupted by greed like so many other women he knew. It wasn't great to realize he'd been wrong, and that she'd probably not be sitting here with him at all if he collected garbage bins. "I guess so," he said gruffly.

Chapter Five

Something had changed, though she couldn't put her finger on *what* that was exactly. She only knew Liam was different somehow, a little more distant, perhaps?

She put down her half-eaten burrito. It was delicious but she was no longer hungry. She did, however, enjoy one more margarita before they pushed back their chairs and headed out to Liam's sports car.

A full moon had slipped free from the concealment of some clouds and it shone down on them brighter than any of the streetlights, lighting Liam's already blond hair as he opened her door.

She nodded thanks, then took her seat, turning to him seconds later as he took the driver's seat to ask, "Where now?"

"Well, that was date one. Date two is coming right up."

It only took another ten minutes before he turned into the parking lot that looked down onto a beach, a salty tang filling her nostrils as waves broke rhythmically against the shore, moonlight reflected in the water.

He parked the car and killed the engine, his voice husky when he asked, "Fancy a walk on the beach?"

She nodded. "I'd love that."

He climbed out and opened her door, and she walked to the steps before she bent and took off her boots while he took off his shoes. They left them on the top step—no one was around to take them—before walking down the concrete steps and onto the gritty, yet soft sand.

"That feels lovely," she said with a sigh. It'd been too long since she'd gone barefooted.

"It does," he acknowledged as he reached for her hand.

She pretended not to notice the electric charge that zapped through her, instead she concentrated on the receding water that rushed back toward them, wetting their feet past their ankles before it receded yet again then repeated the cycle.

She lifted her head into the breeze, admiring the millions of stars scattered like jewels overhead, twinkling high in the velvet sky despite the full moon's brightness. "What is it about the beach that makes worries slip right away?"

"You have a lot of worries?" he asked, his fingers tightening on hers.

She huffed out a dry laugh. "Don't we all?"

"Some more than others," he said, turning to her even while drawing her toward him. "Care to share yours?"

"It's nothing I can't handle," she said dismissively. The last thing she wanted was for their second date to turn into a pity party. She wanted to enjoy this one night with him, not think back about it and cringe.

His eyes assessed her, and though he looked as if he was about to question her, he instead said, "When my brothers and I were just kids, our parents used to book a caravan on the beach every year without fail. We loved fishing and swimming, so our annual holiday was something we always looked forward to."

"Are your parents still around?"

"No. Thanks to a drink driver, they died in a car crash." He looked like he was about to say more, then shook his head and said, "Life was never quite the same after that. It was only lucky us brothers stuck together and did everything we could to make our parents proud."

"I bet they're more than proud of their sons, you're all so successful."

He snorted. "Yeah, well. We discovered early on that money wasn't as hard to make as we thought as long as we put the effort in." He cocked his head to the side. "What about your parents?"

She flinched, then managed a smile. "My mother left me when I was too young to even remember her, and my d-dad," she sucked in a quivery breath, "died almost eighteen months ago to a massive stroke."

"I'm sorry, wildflower. You clearly still miss him."

She nodded. "He was all I had."

Liam drew her into his arms and she savored the closeness, the feeling of sharing the load. She didn't realize she was crying until he stepped back and thumbed dry some of her tears.

She sniffled. "I'm sorry. I didn't mean to ruin the mood—"

"Don't apologize. Of course you still miss your dad. I'm only sorry I didn't get to meet him. He must have been an amazing man to have raised such a wonderful daughter."

She hiccupped. "Now you're j-just being n-nice."

"I'm being honest."

He bent his head and kissed her then, his lips soft and gentle. There was no taking or demanding, he was simply there for her, helping her to forget while creating new memories to hold onto.

She was startled when he pulled back, resentful almost that he'd stopped the one thing that had made her feel better again.

His stare held hers. "I won't take advantage of you."

"You paid for my time," she refuted, her voice wobbly. "You're hardly taking advantage."

The began walking again, the sand squeaking a little under their bare feet and the ocean lulling them with its small swell that hit the sand and rushed over their feet once again before sucking back out to sea.

Liam bent and picked up something. She realized it was a large white shell that looked like a lacy fan. He gave it to her. "Present for you," he said with a flash of white teeth.

She laughed even as she ran her hand over its rough texture. "I'll treasure it."

"Why do I think you really would?" he said huskily, his voice bemused. "I might have paid a quarter million for a night of your time, but it's the shell I think you'll truly appreciate."

She didn't know what to say to that. What *could* she say? That kind of money would save many more horses and benefit her chosen charity in countless ways for a long time. All she'd have was her memories tonight with Liam and the precious shell he'd given her.

She walked with him to some giant boulders that edged the shoreline four hundred meters or so ahead before they turned and headed back the way they'd come. Only once they'd put their footwear back on and he was driving them the way they'd come did she ask, "I'm guessing we're now heading to date number three?"

He nodded. "We are." He glanced at her. "My sister lives not too far away from here. It's up to you if you'd like to borrow some of her clothes or stay in what you have on."

"You have a sister?"

He nodded, then smiled. "I didn't even know myself until a few years ago. But she's everything anyone could ever want in a sibling."

"You love her very much."

He nodded. "Yeah, I do."

He looked contemplative as he drove, and she cleared her throat and looked down at her jeans that were wet just below the knees, sand edging the hems that wrapped around her boots. A good thing the denim wasn't inside her boots, the sand would have rubbed her skin raw.

"You know what, I'm happy to stay in my jeans. I'm comfortable in them and everyone else will just have to accept me wherever we go."

He grinned. "Good answer. No one should ever pretend to be someone they're not."

"It sounds as if you're talking from experience," she said softly.

He cocked a light colored brow. "Let's just say my parents were one thing in front of us boys, but quite another behind our backs. Not that I'm saying there were bad parents by any stretch of the imagination. It was just a...shock to know we'd been lied to."

"And if your parents couldn't be trusted, then who could be?" she deduced.

He sent her a wry smile. "Maybe you're in the wrong business, cowgirl. Maybe counselling should have been your thing."

She laughed. "Maybe you're right." She sobered a little then and confessed, "One day I'd love to help others with emotional issues by using horses to teach them to be calm and grounded. Horses have special abilities in that way."

"I hope you get to see that dream come true."

"Thank you," she said, smiling brightly at him because she perceived he really meant what he said. He wanted her to succeed in her dreams.

She recognized the big building that made up the Black Pearl Nightclub and its function rooms, along with the Garden Café restaurant, its string of lights shining like a beacon on the second level. Then he indicated right and took a ramp that led to a private underground carpark, where a few other priceless cars were parked. No doubt they belonged to the Black brothers.

Parking the car, he climbed out and opened her door, then escorted her toward a private elevator. The doors closed and she shivered even as her blood heated. This was it then. Date number three. No doubt she'd be shown to his bedroom.

That his very presence seemed to suck away the oxygen while he took up all the space just made her more aware of him. He was a magnet and she was a tiny piece of iron compelled to be with him.

Then the doors hissed open and loud music flooded inside the lift, along with rowdy laughter, cheers and the scent of sweat and alcohol. She glanced up at him. "This is date number three?"

He nodded and grinned. "Care to dance?"

Chapter Six

Liam couldn't wipe the smile off his face, not when Harper was beaming as he led her onto the dancefloor and took her in his arms.

Damn, her body pressed to his was all kinds of right.

That his erection probably dug against her wasn't something he could help. It was nothing short of a miracle he'd restrained himself since the auction. He'd never wanted someone half as much as he wanted Harper. She was his every fantasy come to life.

His pulse surged. That she could walk away from him after tonight wasn't something he wanted to think about too hard. For the moment he'd enjoy his time with her.

She looked up at him and mouthed. "Are you okay?"

He nodded, then bent his head so that he was close to her ear and she could hear him above the music. "I'm with you aren't I?" He grinned at the flash in her eyes. "What could possibly be wrong when I'm with you?"

She giggled, then stood on tiptoes to reply. "I bet you say that to all the girls."

He shook his head, then lifted her arm and spun her around, dropping her backward then and catching her so that her head was close to the floor before he answered. "Only you."

The DJ put on a slow song, and he drew her up and against him, then swayed with her around the floor. They fit together perfectly, her curves slotting against his body like she was made for him. He was poetic enough in that moment to believe it was true.

Tomorrow might be a whole other moment for him to contemplate when she walked away. *If* she walked away. He'd never chased a woman in his life, but he'd chase Harper to the ends of the Earth if needed.

Yes, he was cynical and didn't believe in true love. But there was still that hopeful spark inside him that made him wonder *what if.* What if he was wrong and true love really did exist? What if his outlook on the world had been tarnished thanks to the deception of his parents? What if Harper was the one woman on this planet who *was* his soul mate?

His hands tightened their grip on her. She looked up at him with another frown just as Sheikh Korian waltzed past with Fiona, who was still dressed in her skimpy lingerie that enticed men—and some women—into giving generous tips.

Though Fiona was meant to be working, he'd bet Galan and Aiden had given her the night off to be with the sheikh. They were businessmen first and foremost, and Fiona appeared more than happy to be seduced by Korian.

No doubt she'd make a nice bundle out of it.

It only reinforced his earlier thought about Harper. Had she been hoping for Korian to bid on her? She'd been looking at him—enticing him?—when he'd bid on her. She'd seemed more than happy for the sheikh to win.

Yet the delight she'd shown from the shell Liam had given her told him it could have been a diamond for all she'd cared. She was contradictory in so many ways. The sheikh might have given her money and jewels but he would never have thought to have given her something as simple as a shell.

He wouldn't have needed to...

Liam pushed away the thought even as a dark emotion burned through his gut. He stiffened. He would *not* be jealous. He'd never been that type of man before and he had no intention of being one now.

He wasn't the possessive type. He'd left that to his brothers who'd fallen so fast and hard for their women it might have been funny if not for their hearts being on the line.

He glanced around. Speaking of whom...he couldn't see either one of them. But no doubt they'd gone home to their wives. Not that their women were dependent. Galan's wife, Layla, had become a great success as a wedding and events planner, the function rooms booked out well in advance. Aiden's wife, Luna, had started up her own travel agent business and she too was booked solid.

His pulse accelerated. Was it possible he, too, could have it all?

He shoved away the idea. He'd seen what he'd assumed was a great love between his mom and dad. Despite his earlier thoughts, he wasn't foolish enough to believe true love was real. Though his brothers had hit the jackpot, a cynical part of him couldn't help but wonder how long their marriages would last before cracks appeared.

And yet he'd been pining after the same woman for twelve months. Didn't that make him all sorts of a hypocrite?

Harper blinked up at him. "You look like you need a drink?"

He nodded, then smiled and said, "You must be a mind reader."

He drew her toward the bar, where the music was a few decibels quieter. "Vodka and pineapple juice?"

She smiled. "You remembered."

He nodded. "Like it was yesterday."

He ordered her drink and a beer for himself. She accepted hers with a thoughtful look, then said, "If it helps, I couldn't stop thinking about you, either."

He chugged down a couple mouthfuls of his beer, his chest squeezing tight. "Then why did you leave?"

"I came here the first time to check out the auction from a distance. I didn't want or expect any distractions."

His brain whirled. "You saw the sheikh here last year," he said, speaking to himself as much as her. He held her stare. "You really *had* hoped he'd win the bid?"

She shrugged. "It matters little now. You outbid him."

"Was there a reason you wanted him?" he asked, unconsciously holding his breath while waiting for her to reply. Though what he hoped to achieve by hearing it, he had no idea. But then, knowledge was power. Once he knew what he was up against he could engage in battle and tear down her walls, then use his charm to keep them down.

She sucked on her straw, her cheeks hollowing. She put her glass on the bar. "That's...personal."

He narrowed his eyes. She was serious. But it wasn't as if he could pry the truth out of her. His lips curled. There were other, much more fun ways to make her confess. He'd found women wore their hearts on their sleeve after a good lovemaking session.

Lifting his glass to his lips, he swallowed the last of his beer, then *plunked* his glass on the bar right next to hers. Then capturing her chin with one hand, he leaned close and covered her mouth with his, kissing her with something too close to desperation.

She was panting as heavily as him when he finally drew back from her plush lips. He wanted more than to taste her mouth. He wanted to suck on her tits and lick her nipples, he wanted to press kisses along her collarbone while heading south to her pussy where he'd peel her lips apart and suck her tender flesh until she fell apart screaming his name.

Then he'd plunge deep inside her, and claim her as his once and for all. He'd fuck her so hard and diligently that she'd never forget him...never want to walk away. Making her come even harder would be tonight's mission. It would have to be if he wanted to get her to talk openly.

He groaned, his pants suddenly way too constrictive.

She stared up at him with hungry eyes. "Do you think we could get date four underway now?"

"You read my mind again," he growled.

She sniggered. "The only thing I read was the hard-on tenting your pants."

He was too aroused to laugh at her honesty. "Let's get out of here," he said thickly. Then encircling his arm around her waist, he drew her toward the elevator that would take them to his private residence.

Chapter Seven

Harper was flushed, burning for Liam by the time they stepped into the elevator. The doors slid closed. As they ascended, their fingers stayed intertwined, but they didn't otherwise touch each other. If they did, they wouldn't be getting out of the elevator anytime soon.

It seemed like an eternity before the elevator doors swished back open, revealing a generous sitting room. It was a living space all of its own with its buttery leather lounges, big screen television and potted plants, not to mention the tinted windows with superb views.

Liam swept a hand toward the three doors set into alcoves. "Each of us brothers has our own penthouse suite." He laughed softly. "Not that Galan or Aiden stay here often anymore. Despite their wives enjoying it here, my brothers enjoy even more having their privacy. "

Harper imagined marriage would have seen Liam's brothers more than willing to give up their former bachelor pads for private living arrangements. Her heart squeezed like a fist. What would it feel like to have a man like Liam want to reform and give up his playboy lifestyle?

Her breath shuddered out. Why was she even contemplating such a thing? He had his life here, which was far removed from the life she intended to have in the country. She had her own dreams, her own future that didn't include a man like Liam, a man whose intent had been clear from the start—to have the one woman who'd gotten away.

What had he'd said? *And this time we're finishing what we started.*

That he could afford the amount he'd bid on her still blew her mind. Not even Sheikh Korian had denied Liam what—*who*—he'd so clearly wanted.

He drew her with him past the leather lounges and toward a door on the right. But his hand holding hers was no longer enough, she needed more of him. He reached for the handle of his door set inside its niche just as she reached up and touched his nape.

He froze, then turned around as if in slow motion. No words were needed, the energy and lust throbbing between them was more than enough. Neither of them could deny what they wanted.

He put his hand behind her neck in return, then pulled her to him. Their lips met and their breaths merged, and he slid his hands up and down her back as he kissed her liked there was no tomorrow and now was all they had together.

Now *was* all they had, she had no illusions there would be more than his bid that had brought them together. It didn't mean she couldn't enjoy every minute of their time together.

He unbuttoned her blouse and all but ripped it off her even as she pushed his jacket over his shoulders, then dragged the sleeves free from his arms, his shirt following soon after. He cursed as he fumbled with the clasp on her bra before tossing it aside and freeing her breasts. His eyes glowed as he stared at her. "You're fucking perfect."

Her heart lodged in her throat. She'd heard plenty of empty praises in the past, but Liam meant what he said. His eyes all but glowed with worship as he reverently cupped her breasts and tweaked her nipples, creating a burn of need to pulse through her, his skilled touch making her realize just how experienced he was compared to her handful of past lovers.

He released her then as she tugged off her boots, then he reached for her to undo her jeans button and zipper before he dragged her denim and lacy panties all the way to her ankles. She stepped out of them as he pulled a foil from out of his pants, then thrust the fabric down along with his boxer briefs.

Her insides twisted then did a frightened little jig as she stared at his cock. *Holy crap.* He was definitely extra-large. She might be wet but she wasn't *that* wet. She'd need lube, and lots of it.

His eyes burned into hers as he rolled the condom onto the considerable length of his cock. "I can't wait one second longer," he growled thickly.

She gaped. There was no way he'd fit.

He reached down, his thumb pressing on her clit before he rotated it so that her nerve endings fired into life, her gasp morphing into a moan as pleasure streaked through her and wetness soaked her thighs.

"Neither can I," she said shakily.

He didn't need to be told twice. He spun her around so that her spine pressed against the door. Then lifting her so that she wrapped her ankles around his hips, he said hoarsely, "Hang on tight."

There was no time to deny him entry, no time to even consider a change of mind. He thrust his full length inside her and she gasped at the burning stretch of her inner muscles. *Damn.* He might be too big for her near-virginal muscles, but she no longer doubted why the Black brothers we so in demand by the ladies.

A muscle ticked in his jaw. "Tell me you're all right?"

She nodded stiffly, then lied, "Of course."

His eyes flared, and he paused for a microsecond. Then he pulled out of her most of the way before he slammed back in. She closed her eyes. *Oh, fuck.* He didn't seriously expect her to enjoy sex with him when he was so well-endowed. Did he?

Every time he plunged inside her the friction lit her from the inside out, but the burn soon became a smolder and then a wildfire. Her body was no longer objecting his entry, it welcomed him. She had no idea when she'd started meeting him thrust for thrust, but suddenly she was swept away in the whirlpool of pleasure, her pleasure building faster and faster—

She threw her head back and cried out something incomprehensible, her body shuddering as an orgasm took away all thought while sensation overcome her, throwing her high and burning her up like a shooting star. Colors flashed as she soared and she was distantly aware of Liam's low, piercing growl as he too succumbed to pleasure, his seed pulsing.

Ping.

Her eyes went wide and latched onto Liam's.

He blinked. "Shit. The elevator's gone back to ground level. One of my brothers must still be here."

She blinked, but otherwise it was as if she was caught in a web and she couldn't move. "What do we do?"

He snorted, then kissed her hard before he withdrew carefully from her. "We get into my penthouse—fast."

He placed her onto her feet, and somehow their passion dissolved into fits of laughter as they grabbed their clothes and shoved open the door, stumbling inside before slamming the door shut again.

They were still laughing when Liam drew her into his bedroom. She lay on the bed, and he turned serious as he bent and kissed her again. His eyes glowing, he said huskily, "Don't go anywhere, wildflower. I need to dispose of this condom so I can fill another. But not before I feast on your delectable pussy."

*

Harper woke slowly, luxuriating in having Liam's strong arms wrapped around her as his hard body spooned her, his bare skin warm against hers. She savored it—for just a moment—before she carefully extricated herself from his clasp.

All the while she ignored the voice screaming inside her head to stay, to linger for even just a few moments longer. Except those minutes might well turn into hours and she was fighting the need to leave hard enough already.

Pulling on her underwear and then her jeans and top, she glanced one last time at the man who'd brought her whole body alive. His blond hair gleamed in the dawn light that streamed through the window, his bare ass slightly whiter than the rest of his body.

He mumbled something in his sleep, then reached for her, somehow staying asleep even as he groaned in denial at her absence.

Shit. It was time to go.

She couldn't do an awkward goodbye. Best to go like a wraith in the early morning, and leave him sleep off his big night. She smiled. He'd been ravenous and hadn't fallen asleep until an hour or so before the crack of dawn.

"Goodbye, Liam," she said softly.

Touching her jeans pocket to make sure her shell was still inside; she walked out of his bedroom and toward the door that led into the sitting room. She had yet to grab her clutch bag and car keys from the locker in the conference room. Luckily she and the other girls had been informed they had access to the lockers until midday the next day after the auction.

It wasn't until she pressed the elevator button and the doors slid open with the slightest hiss that a weight lifted off her shoulders.

She was free.

She pressed a hand to her stomach. That there was a hard lump inside meant little. She'd miss Liam a whole lot more this time around. Though she might have also missed out on the money needed to make her bed and breakfast a reality, it didn't mean there weren't any other options. She'd work hard at turning the vision she and her dad had had into reality.

Perhaps work would be the one way she might eventually forget about the man who'd pleasured her so thoroughly.

Or perhaps she was delusional and she'd yet to accept wishes were for fools and dreams didn't always come true.

Chapter Eight

Liam opened his eyes with a harsh exhale.

He was alone.

He sat and peered around the room, his breath quietening as he listened for any sound outside his bedroom. "Harper?"

Nothing.

But he'd known that even before he'd called out her name. Her clothes that she'd left scattered across the floor entangled with his were gone.

He reached for his cell, his heart thumping in his chest.

"Hello," a voice rasped that was rusty with sleep.

"Justin," he greeted. He didn't bother with pleasantries or an apology for the earliness of his call. He paid Justin well for his PI skills. "How did you go with the information I requested?"

"About the girl, Harper Franks?"

"Who else?" Liam growled.

Justin chuckled, seemingly wide awake now. "I'll have all the information you need emailed to you within five minutes. Will that be all for now?"

Liam squeezed his cell, then said, "Thank you. That's all."

Their call disconnected and Liam pushed to his feet and headed toward the bathroom. He'd have a shower and clear his head, then he'd get dressed and pack a suitcase, ready to leave the moment he uncovered her address and everything else he needed to know about Harper Franks.

Fifteen minutes later, he was on the road driving west of Sydney, the buildings, houses and shops soon giving way to trees and farmland. Cows and horses grazed the land, eucalyptus a pungent and heavy scent in the air.

His thoughts weren't so much on the scenery though as they were on the woman who'd distracted him beyond measure. He was becoming damn-well obsessed with her!

One night hadn't eased his need for her, it had increased it. The fact she'd left without saying goodbye had cut deeper than he wanted to admit. They were good together—why couldn't *she* see that?

Either way, he wasn't giving up without a fight. He'd do everything in his power to convince her to take a chance on them.

He flicked his indicator on and turned right into a thinner strip of sealed road, a caravan and shed set deep into the trees on the corner block. A handful of fluffy white clouds scudded across the sky overhead, a flock of rainbow lorikeets a blur of color as they flew across the road just ahead and settled into a huge flowering gum tree.

His thoughts drifted again. His private investigator had sent him some interesting and in-depth information. Though he'd known Harper's father had died around eighteen months ago, Liam hadn't known her dad had also left her in a whole lot of debt thanks to a crippling mortgage on a property that she paid minimum repayments on.

He hadn't needed to be a genius to realize he'd been right all along. She'd banked on the sheikh winning the bid and ultimately giving her a wad of money as a bonus just for being with him. That she'd not even hinted for money from Liam dented his ego. Had she been too proud to tell him the truth? Or had she presumed he'd spent all his fortune already on his bid for her?

Hadn't he proven his worth?

He glanced at his GPS and flicked on his indicator again to turn left, leaving the sealed road to travel along a dusty track that was more suited to tractors than cars. A kangaroo bounded across the road in front of him and he swore as he slammed on his brakes. He should have taken his Range Rover but he'd had no idea Harper lived in what seemed like the middle of nowhere.

He glanced at his clock. She was actually a little under an hour away from where he lived, and yet it seemed as though the city was a million miles away.

A rickety barbed wire fence appeared ahead either side of a cattle grid. He went over it, his whole car vibrating. He was on her property now, he was certain of it.

He slowed the car as potholes appeared on the road, the trees either side thick and tall, their canopy shading much of the road. Then the trees as quickly gave way to a clearing.

To the left, rotting cattle yards and a weed-infested paddock looked even worse with new railed paddocks to the right showcasing lush green grass. Two chestnut horses and a gray happily grazed next to a lake that glinted under the sun, the vines of a weeping willow touching its water.

Heading over a rise, the two-storied, sprawling white-fading-to-gray house that had probably been a mansion in its prime was now nothing short of a crumbling disaster. He frowned. If that really was her home, it was clear now why she'd needed financial help.

Then he spotted her white SUV and his frown turned into a relieved smile. He'd found her.

Chapter Nine

Harper turned off the hose she'd been using to give her organic vegetables a drink, turning then to watch the low slung sports car as it approached. That it was Liam's car registered long before the joy suffusing her from the inside out did.

What was wrong with her? She should be angry. He was invading her private property, her personal space! A pity it didn't wipe the smile off her face.

She stalked around the side of her house toward him, swatting at the fly buzzing around her head. She'd never given Liam her address, she'd never even hinted at where she lived. "Yet here he is," she muttered.

It was amazing what one could find out when money was freely available. She grimaced as she watched the sports car brake to a stop, a cloud of dust billowing over it. Even covered in filth it'd never fully belong to a place like this...just as Liam would never fully belong to a woman like her.

So what was he doing here?

Then he climbed out of his car and all her questions and good intentions fled. He looked like rain on a hot summer's day, like bare feet dancing on a plush green meadow filled with spring flowers.

She caught herself from running to him and instead used her most haughty voice to state, "It hasn't even been twenty-four hours since I left."

He peeled his sunglasses off his face, the dark blond bristles on his jaw somehow enhancing his slick, city look. His blue stare caught and held hers. "And yet I miss you already, wildflower." He cocked his head to the side. "I'd hoped you might be a little happier to see me."

She looked down at her dirt-stained denim shorts and gray T-shirt, her canvas shoes with the holes in their toes. Compared to his khaki cargo pants and bright white T-shirt, he could have stepped straight off a Milan runway.

She cleared her throat and looked back at him, his gaze now assessing her, as though reading her every thought, her every doubt. She narrowed her eyes. "I fulfilled my part of the contract."

He threw his sunglasses onto his driver's seat and shut the door with a *thunk*. "You did," he acknowledged. "But did you really think one night was ever going to be enough for us?"

"For us?" she repeated, swallowing past her suddenly dry throat. How many times on her drive home had she nearly turned back and returned to him? She'd lost count. Only self-preservation and a will of iron had seen her drive straight to her place...her future.

It took everything she had to put steel in her voice. "I thought I made it more than apparent when I left you and didn't look back that there was no *us*?"

He crossed his arms, his jaw tightening. "You made it more than clear." His blue eyes that looked back at her were just as steely. "But I hope you'll at least consider giving us another chance."

She fisted her hands, her nails breaking the skin of her palms. "Why would you even want a chance with a girl like me?" Damn it, she didn't want to sound...needy, like she had to have his reassurances just to make her feel worthy of him.

"I think the more obvious question is why I wouldn't? I did, after all, bid a quarter million on you."

She lifted her chin. "I never asked you to spend that kind of money on me, though I'm sure my charity would kiss your toes if you asked them to knowing how many more horses they can now save." But for how long, though? The feed and medicines alone were staggering.

"I'm glad your charity is happy, I really am. But what about *our* happiness, Harper?"

She blinked at his use of her real name. It was odd how quickly she'd gotten used to his *wildflower* endearment, how much she enjoyed hearing it from his lips.

He inhaled, then added softly, "All that I ask for now is a conversation."

She nodded. She hadn't exactly been gracious to him, not considering he'd done everything right by her. "Then we'd best go inside out of this hot sun." She stepped toward the cracked pavers that were a pathway to her front door. "This way."

She tilted her chin a little higher. She would *not* be humbled by the state of her abode. One day she'd have this whole property looking as majestic as it'd once been. That she'd also be earning coin from it was just a bonus.

She opened the screen door, ignoring the rips in it as she stepped inside onto worn, brown and gold linoleum. He followed her in and she shut the door behind her, squeezing her eyes closed for a second in irritation as the pesky fly flew straight through the screen door with them.

Exhaling slowly, she pivoted to face him and asked, "So...coffee?"

"Just iced water would be great, thanks."

Her smile was probably more gritted teeth than anything as she conceded, "I don't have a freezer at the moment, only a fridge."

"Then cold water will be fine," he said mildly, as though not affected by her lack of conveniences.

He probably thought she was a savage. A country bumpkin who lacked the finer graces he'd expect from a woman.

She stalked into the kitchen. Though it was ancient, there were plenty of drawers and cupboards for storage. That it was a frightful orange color had never really bothered her before and she refused to let it bother her now. She walked around the island bench then opened her refrigerator door to pull out the bottle of water inside, pouring them a glass each.

"We'll probably be more comfortable in the lounge room," she said. It was the one room on the ground level she was proud of, a room she'd done just for herself, not her future guests.

He followed her as she walked past the dining room with its huge table and twelve chairs before she opened up bi-fold doors. Waiting for him to step into the room, she shut the doors behind them before turning on a little portable air conditioner that struggled valiantly against the heat whenever she used it.

She managed a smile that was probably more a grimace. "One day I'll get ducted air conditioning. Until then, this little unit should keep us a little cooler."

He sipped on his water and glanced approvingly around the room. "I applaud your designer, he—*she*?—has done an amazing job in here."

She followed his gaze to the billowy lace curtains and the navy drapes tied back either side of large twin windows, and the painted navy walls with white trim and high, white ceilings. She particularly loved the large portrait on the wall of her late father, along with the collection of smaller framed photos assembled around it, mostly of her and her dad fishing, horse riding and camping.

"No designer did this," she said in a soft voice. "That huge vase in the corner was my grandmother's. The dried grasses in it were the first things my dad and I dug up after we purchased this place. They were meant to be a souvenir to remind us later that our hard work had been worth it." A tear rolled down her cheek. She swiped at it. "It's a reminder now of what my father and I shared...and what I still hope to achieve."

"Christ, Harper. I had no idea."

She shook her head and said brokenly, "No one does. It was just my father and me. And this place is his legacy, one I plan to bring back to life, even if I can't ever do the same for him."

Chapter Ten

Liam's chest expanded as her pain became his pain. She hadn't finished grieving, not by a long shot. And he wasn't even sure it was just her father that she mourned. She'd lost her mother, too. The only difference was that her mother was likely still alive.

Either way, it was obvious this property was steeped in memories and emotions for Harper, her heart attached to this place she called home.

"You've never thought about finding your mother?" he asked gently.

She shook her head. "Why would I want to find someone who doesn't want to be found? She didn't just leave her husband; she left her only child, her own flesh and blood." Her breath shuddered out. "I don't know about you, but to me that's unforgiveable."

He grimaced. Not even his own father had disowned his illegitimate daughter from an affair no one except Galan and their mom had known about. His parents' marriage might have made a mockery of their vows, but the love they'd had for their children hadn't been a lie. If he believed in nothing else, he had to believe that.

"You're right, it *is* unforgiveable. But do you know what is even more unforgiveable?'

She shook her head as he stepped toward her, his conviction burning the edges of his vision. "Holding onto the rejection and abandonment you have for your mother, and allowing your emotions to cripple you from trusting anyone else." He cocked his head to one side. "Including me."

She blinked. "That's not true."

"Isn't it? You ran from me just like your mom ran from you," he said softly, but with such loud intent it thrummed the very atmosphere of the room.

She took a step back, then gritted, "I'm nothing like my mother."

"Prove it then," he said, stepping toward her. "Show me you're not scared to take a chance on us."

She crossed her arms, adopting a defensive position. "I don't need to prove anything to anyone. Least of all to a man I had sex with for one night only."

Her words were like a punch to his gut. But he wasn't without his own weapons. "Tell me one night was enough for you and I'll walk away right now and not look back."

Her eyes flashed, then she blinked away the need he'd glimpsed and covered it with distrust. "That's not fair."

"Life often isn't."

He and his brothers had learned that lesson, as had she. That she was also fighting to make something of her life, just like he and his brothers had, was just as evident.

If only she'd let him help her. He'd love to pay it forward. After all, he had all the money in his bank account to make her present situation less stressful. But he doubted that she'd thank him for the offer. Though she mightn't have had any issue taking money from Sheikh Korian, he'd bet she'd have an issue taking it from Liam.

He wasn't the stranger she'd expected. They'd had a year of thinking and dreaming about one another, a year before they were reunited once again, their chemistry heightened thanks to their absence.

"You don't need to tell me that," she conceded, her arms then dropping to her sides. "But this place makes me happier. It's...sacred ground."

"And I'm an intruder," he finished softly.

She nodded. "Yes." She looked away. "No. That isn't what I meant. All I really know is that my dream, my future, is all wrapped up in this place and there's no room for anyone else."

"You can make room," he said gently. "No one needs to go through life on their own. There isn't any harm in sharing dreams."

She turned to him, her eyes flashing again. "You say that as though you'd enjoy laboring here to make this place something special again."

He shrugged. "Who said I wouldn't?" At her silence, he added, "Don't judge me by my suit. I worked hard with my brothers to make the Black Pearl Nightclub, its restaurant and function rooms the success they are. I've worked as hard on my own projects to make them just as prosperous in their own right."

She winced. "I've always prided myself on never judging a book by its cover. To be honest, I thought it would be you judging me."

"No. For too many years other people judged us Black brothers—judged our parents—and found fault thanks to all the rumors swirling around." His laugh was as dark as those memories. "It taught me a valuable lesson."

Her stare darkened with questions, but she ignored them. For the moment she seemed as focused on their relationship, if it could be called that, as he was. "What lesson was that?" she asked.

"Not to judge others in return."

She bit her bottom lip, but this time she took a step toward him. His heart throbbed with hope. It was like cornering a wild animal, then holding out a hand as it tentatively sniffed, earning its trust. "I shouldn't have doubted you," she said.

When she stopped in front of him and lifted her arms to encircle his neck, he couldn't stop a growl of longing as he cupped her face and their mouths met in mutual accord. He was instantly lost in the moment, her lips pillowing his as something magical pulsated between them and escalated fast.

She pulled back, her eyes wary even as she breathed heavily with need. "This isn't right."

His vision distorted at the edges as desire continued to burn inside him. "Tell me it's wrong?"

She bit her bottom lip. "I can't."

"Then stop overthinking. Some things are just meant to be."

She squeezed her eyes closed. "Perhaps you're right."

"I know I am," he said huskily.

Surely she couldn't deny their chemistry?

She didn't.

Flicking off the air conditioner, she took hold of his hand and led him from the lounge room to a bedroom on the ground level that appeared to be self-contained.

Then all his peripheral awareness faded as he became lost in the moment with her.

Chapter Eleven

Liam woke feeling as content and relaxed as he'd ever been. There was something to be said about lovemaking and fresh country air. A magpie warbled outside the window as though serenading them, its song making him smile.

Except, he was already smiling. He'd succeeded in winning over Harper, at least in bed, now he had to win over her heart. Anything less was unacceptable.

Though he was tempted to wake her by burying his dick between her thighs once again, he resisted the idea and instead climbed out of bed. She'd need her sleep after he'd woken her three times to enjoy her body while bringing her to orgasmic bliss.

She rolled onto her back, muttering something incomprehensible, then she relaxed and breathed evenly once again as she slipped back into a deep sleep. He paused, looking down at her tanned arms on top of the white bed sheets, her strawberry-blonde hair in disarray around her head and the globes of her perfect breasts that were half-exposed.

He swallowed back an urge to uncover her completely and stare at her perfection, but that wasn't a gentlemanly thing to do. He was here to earn her trust, not take it away.

He stalked into her bathroom, all but wincing at the ghastly green-faded-to-yellow tiles. He'd bet Harper normally woke up at the crack of dawn, it'd do her good to sleep in.

After indulging in a quick, hot shower—she might rely solely on tank water—he wrapped a towel around his hips and went outside to grab his bag from out of his car.

He had three changes of clothes. It should be enough time to sway Harper's mindset about him. If not, he could always use her washing machine and stay a little longer.

After getting dressed into shorts and a cream and gold T-shirt, he went into her kitchen and filled an electric kettle with water, then flicked it on before he searched her pantry for coffee. He found a jar of instant, his brow furrowing.

Not because of the cheap coffee. He couldn't help but notice how very little of anything else she had in stock. Five cans of cat food, a small bag of flour, salt and pepper, some potatoes and onions in a basket, a can of pineapple pieces and a tin of apricot nectar.

He made a mental note to order more groceries for her just as a cat pushed against the back of his legs and gave a pitiful meow.

He bent and stroked a hand over the tabby fluffball, its feather duster of a tail making him smirk. "I bet you just hang around expecting treats and pats all day without doing any work to earn them."

"Mrowww."

"Yeah, that's what I thought."

He reached for the closest tin of cat food and undone its ring-pull before he followed the trotting cat into the laundry where its dish was located. He poured the food and watched as the cat gobbled it down as though it was its first ever meal.

He smirked as he returned to the kitchen and disposed of the can into the trash. At least Harper wasn't completely alone here.

"I see you've met Tibbles."

He swung around, his eyes widening and his pulse escalating at seeing Harper. Though her gorgeous body was concealed thanks to a bathrobe, it didn't impede her sexy vibe. With her hair sticking out from where he'd dug his fingers through it, her face flushed and her brown-gold eyes glowing.

Little wonder. He'd lost count of how many times she'd shattered beneath him.

He managed a chuckle even as his dick thickened and expanded once again. She was truly a vision, one he'd love to wake up to every morning. He cleared his throat and focused on her query. "If Tibbles is the tabby cat I just fed, then yes, I most definitely have."

She glanced toward the laundry. "He would have been distraught that I'd missed his early morning breakfast." She smirked. "But it seems he's trained you in my stead."

"Enslaved to the cat." He shook his head. "I never thought I'd see that day." He sobered a little, aware there was much to be said before she decided to get rid of him and go back to just the company of her cat. "Mind if we talk?" he asked. He nodded toward the instant coffee he'd dragged out of the pantry. "I was making us coffee."

She looked down and rubbed the back of her neck. "What do you want to talk about?"

"Us." He found some cups and put two on the countertop before he spooned in the coffee. "Milk and sugar?" he asked.

"Just milk, thank you." She thrust a hand through her hair, her lips twisting a little. "I feel like that is something you should know.'

"How you like your coffee?"

She nodded. "It's as if I've been sleeping with a stranger."

He stirred milk into her coffee, keeping his voice neutral. "It would have been that way no matter who won the bid."

"Unless I chose not to sleep with any other man who did."

He placed the teaspoon into the sink even as a jagged flash of something too close to envy slid through his bloodstream, leaving behind a toxic note. "If the sheikh had won would you have slept with him?"

She accepted the coffee he handed her. "He didn't win, so it's a moot point."

"But he wanted you. And you wanted him."

Her knuckles whitened on the cup handle. "I never said I wanted him."

"It was pretty clear from where I was standing that you hoped he'd win." He picked up his cup and acted bland while inside he hid a noxious mess of emotions. He took a sip and resisted wincing. He'd gotten too used of the freshest coffee bean blends. "When I won, you all but froze on the stage."

She blinked. "That's because I hadn't imagined anyone bidding that insane amount on me."

"Not because you'd banked on the fact the sheikh would win?" he asked hoarsely, his throat dry.

She put her untouched coffee down. "What does it matter now?" she said with narrowed eyes. "You won me. The sheikh lost. End of story."

He exhaled slowly. "You're right. It's time I moved on."

"It is," she agreed.

For fuck's sake. He was acting like he owned her. He reached out and cupped her chin, his thumb stroking. "I'm sorry." Her lashes swept low, and with a rough growl he leaned in and kissed her, a gentle reminder of how good they were together.

His cell chose that moment to chime from somewhere in the bedroom. He stepped back reluctantly and said, "I'd better answer that."

She nodded and smiled. "You probably should."

He stalked into her bedroom and pulled his cell out of his cargo pants he'd abandoned hastily last night on the floor. "Liam speaking."

"Liam, it's Aiden."

"Aiden," Liam said in return, his chest tightening in premonition as his brother exhaled harshly. "What's up?"

"It's our sister." Aiden paused, then said roughly, "Sienna's been hurt. A car accident. She's in hospital now."

"*What?*"

"I can't tell you any of the details, right now you know as much as I do. I'm on my way to the hospital now."

His pulse drummed in his ears. "I'll be there in an hour."

He disconnected the call, his mind blank for a handful of seconds as he tried to process it all. His sister was hurt, possibly seriously injured. His vision distorted. He'd had such a short time getting to know his sister, he couldn't lose her now.

But he couldn't deny that his parents were taken from him in a car crash. It was history repeating itself.

"Liam, what is it?"

He shook his head, unable to articulate any words. What could he say?

"Liam? You're scaring me."

He dragged a hand over his face, trying to focus on the woman in front of him, the woman who was staring at him with glittering eyes in a white face. "I-I have to go," he said numbly. "My sister has been in a-a car accident."

She stepped forward, her arms wrapping around him. "I'm sorry." She stepped back, blinking up at him. "You're in shock. You can't drive in that state." She stepped back. "I'll drive you."

Chapter Twelve

Harper pulled into the front entrance of the hospital's emergency department. Liam swung open the door and, halfway to climbing out, he paused and turned around. "You're not coming in?"

Her heart palpitated even as she threw him a bright smile. "This is a private matter between you and your family." She swallowed hard. "I'll go back to your penthouse and wait for you there. Ring me when you need me to pick you up again."

He blinked at her, then nodded and climbed out, shutting the passenger door without a word. She bit her bottom lip as she watched him stride away, his usually smooth, predatory steps looking stiff and wooden.

She resisted jumping out of the car and running after him, resisted trying to support him when he was so clearly vulnerable. But what was she to him, really? She'd been his lover for exactly two nights. They might not be strangers physically, but they very much were in every other way.

He had his brothers there to console him.

So why was her heart so heavy when she pulled back out onto the road and drove back to the building where he lived? Damn it, she'd been second-guessing everything since Liam had come into her life, and her feelings—and his—were at the top of that heap.

She was blessedly numb by the time she turned into the underground parking lot. A minute later she stepped into the elevator, gripping her clutch bag as she ascended smoothly to the top of the building.

She stepped into the sitting room that Liam shared with his brothers, then threw herself onto one of its buttery lounges. Who had she been kidding? She couldn't possibly go into Liam's penthouse alone. If she couldn't support him by visiting his sister in the hospital with him, she most certainly didn't deserve to enter his home.

She didn't belong here.

She ran trembling fingers up and down her legs, wishing then she'd thrown on one of her everyday pair of jeans. Instead she'd chosen a white mini-skirt, a pink button-up blouse and white boots.

The longer she sat the more she berated herself, her eyes becoming gritty from forcing back tears. Liam deserved better. She was no good for him, now or in the future.

She pushed to her feet. She needed something strong to drink, but she'd settle for a coffee. It was something of a relief to find a seat in the open air Garden Café Restaurant, where a balding man brought her the coffee she'd requested and put it down in front of her along with a muffin.

He smiled at her, his bushy, silver eyebrows drawn together. "I brought you one of my famous choc-chip muffins—on the house," he added. "You looked like you might need some comfort food."

"Thank you." She smiled at him, his kind gesture undoing some of the tight knots inside.

He took a step back and beamed. "You're welcome, young lady."

"Please, call me Harper."

"Ah." He nodded sagely. "You're the woman Liam bid on."

"How did you know?"

He chuckled. "You mean besides hearing your name just now? Your hair was a bit of a giveaway. There aren't too many strawberry blondes around here."

She touched some of the loose ends. She should have worn her hair up, but she'd barely had time to get dressed and organize for her neighbor to feed Tibbles once again. "I guess you'd hear a lot of gossip."

He nodded. "Folks like to talk, especially the staff. If they can't find anything inflammatory about one other, they like nothing better than to gossip about their notorious bosses." He pushed a hand over his bald head. "Most of the women who work here have had a crush on at least one of the brothers. Being that Liam was the last bachelor...well, let's just say there were a lot of disappointed sighs."

She shook her head. "Liam is a free agent."

"Is he?"

She took a sip of her coffee. Damn, there was nothing like specially blended and freshly ground coffee beans to lift her spirits. She put her cup back down, then looked at the man who appeared to have doubts about Liam's bachelor status. "I'm nothing more to him than a passing interest."

"Then I guess that makes you a free agent, too?"

She jerked her head around, her eyes widening at seeing the suave man behind her. "Sheikh Korian! I-I didn't realize you were here."

He smiled. "It wasn't my intention to scare you." He nodded at the seat opposite her. "Do you mind?"

"No. No, of course not. Please, take a seat."

"You're too kind," Korian said with an even wider smile. He nodded at the bald man who appeared frozen in place. "Hi Ned, I'll have what she's having."

"Of course," the other man—Ned—said, bowing a little before he turned and hurried back to the café hut.

Korian turned his attention back to her. "I hope I'm not being presumptuous here, but if I'd won that bid I would never have let you out of my sight."

"The bid was only for one night," she reminded him.

"And yet you're still here."

She nodded. "Liam had some...personal stuff come up."

If he and his brothers wanted to talk about their sister's car accident that was up to them, not her.

Korian cocked a dark brow. "And he didn't insist you stay by his side? Interesting."

She ignored a sharp flare of annoyance. Being a sheikh he was probably used to people bowing and scraping to him. He wouldn't be getting that from her. "I'm not sure how things work in your country, Sheikh Korian, but over here we value our freedom. I chose to be alone and Liam respected that decision."

That he'd probably also been hurt by it was her burden to carry.

The sheikh laughed. "My, oh my, you really are refreshing. I can see why Liam bid so high on you. My only regret now is that I didn't double his offer."

She lifted her chin. "I'm sure my charity would have appreciated that very much."

"But not you so much?"

"I never said that."

"You didn't have to, Harper. Not everyone is as fortunate as me. I have enough funds to keep me going for many lifetimes."

"I'm glad you realize how blessed you are."

"Indeed." He lifted a hand that had to be heavy with all his chunky gold rings. "Perhaps that is why I enjoy sharing my wealth around."

She lifted her cup to her lips and drank her hot coffee in a couple of big gulps. That it scalded her throat barely registered. All she could focus on was what the sheikh hinted at. "Oh?"

He plucked a napkin off the table and leaned across the table to dab at the coffee she'd left on one corner of her lip. "I have a proposition for you," he said softly.

She leaned back, wary now. "I'm...listening."

"You intrigued me from the start," he conceded. "So I did a little digging." He put his hands up at her outraged gasp. "Nothing too deep, just enough to know you're looking for investors for your future bed and breakfast."

"And if I am?"

"If you are...I'm willing to invest."

Holy shit. All her dreams and aspirations were being answered! But was it all too good to be true? "What's the catch?"

"Must there be one?" he asked.

"There's *always* one."

He clucked his tongue. "So cynical for such a young woman."

"Being alone does that to a person."

It was only then she realized how contrary she sounded. She wanted her freedom by being alone while berating the fact she *was* alone.

"I'm here, aren't I?" He sat back. "Not that I can say the same for the youngest Black brother." He gave her a crooked smile. "No matter how much you might enjoy your freedom, if I was him I'd never let you out of my sight."

Korian nodded at Ned as he placed his coffee and muffin on the table in front of the sheikh. The moment he was gone, Korian returned his attention to Harper. "So tell me, are you interested in me investing in your business?"

Goose bumps sprang up on her arms. "What are you suggesting, exactly?"

"How does half-a-million dollars sound to get your property up and running within the next twelve months?"

She sucked in a breath, reeling by his generous offer. "And the catch?" she finally prompted.

"That is your choice. Half-a-million to date me for a week and sleep with me every night, whip included."

Her stomach crunched. She was desperate, but she wasn't *that* desperate. One night of losing a piece of herself had been one thing, but a whole week?

She cleared her throat. "And my other choice?"

"Half a million in advance. Then fifty percent of the profits are mine for the next ten years."

She gaped. It was like being caught between a rock and a hard place. Seven days of no doubt sickening sexual acts or the next ten years of her life giving this man fifty percent of her hard earned profits? But without his half-million would she even have a business?

And what about Liam? Does he get any say in this?

A shiver went up and down her spine that she even considered his feelings in her future. He was as likely to walk away from her as everyone else in her life had. Only her dad had stuck around and even he'd died on her thanks to his stroke.

She lifted her chin. This was her life, her fight. "I'd need to see both options in writing before even considering signing either one of them."

He nodded. "Of course, I wouldn't expect anything less from an astute business woman."

"There may be...negotiations."

His eyes flashed, anger then superseded by admiration. "I'll have something written up for you in a few hours." He stood, then reached over and took her closest hand in his. He lifted it to his mouth and kissed the back of her knuckles. "I look forward to doing business with you."

She frowned. She hadn't signed any contract yet, but he clearly thought she wouldn't refuse. What sane woman would?

"Business?" Liam asked behind her.

Sheikh Korian smirked. "Business hopefully mixed with pleasure." He held her hand a little longer than necessary and said, "Your decision, Harper." Then he released her and walked away, his coffee and muffin left untouched.

Chapter Thirteen

Liam felt broken, betrayed. Destroyed.

Harper pushed to her feet, her face flushed and her golden-brown eyes glittering. She'd never looked more damn beautiful. "Liam. H-how is your sister?"

"Besides two broken ribs, a broken leg and a whole lot of cuts and bruises, she's in remarkably good spirits." Unlike him. "But there's no need for you to pretend to care now."

She gaped, her big brown-gold eyes wounded. "That's a horrible thing to say," she whispered.

"I guess the truth hurts."

He knew his emotions were taking over and careening him down a path he didn't want to take, but he was a freight train without brakes and he couldn't stop even if he wanted to.

"I'm glad your sister is okay." She pushed to her feet, her eyes wet. "But I'm done here now," she said, her voice wobbly. "*We're* done."

His heart cramped as his soul withered. "I guess that means you're free now to go to the sheikh," he ground out. "How very convenient for you."

To think he'd been ready to give her everything, including his heart, to make her happy. Though he didn't doubt for a second she'd be successful with or without his help in time, he'd just wanted to speed up the process for her. He knew how hard it was to get a business off the ground, and he'd had two brothers by his side.

Harper was alone.

No. Not alone. She had Korian now.

She held his stare, her cheeks flushed and her eyes filled with sorrow. "Goodbye, Liam."

He didn't stop her when she turned and walked out of his life. He was too busy pretending he wasn't breaking into a thousand jagged little pieces.

He was still standing looking after her long after she'd gone when Ned approached, supposedly to clean off the table, though he felt the other man's eyes on him.

"Such a waste," Ned mused as he picked up the two uneaten muffins and one untouched coffee. He looked at Liam. "Are you okay?"

"I've been better," Liam admitted in a colorless voice. "But life goes on, right?"

Ned frowned as he placed the coffee and muffins back on the table. "You mean to say you're giving up on that lovely young lady? She deserves better than that sheikh. No doubt he's trying to buy her off with all his unlimited funds." He shook his head. "I only hope she's smart enough not to fall for it."

"She's certainly smart enough, which is why I think she will be bought."

Ned shook his head. "I hope you're wrong, I really do. Korian would ruin her."

Liam had heard enough. "Then that's on her."

He walked away with Ned gaping after him. What Ned didn't understand was that Harper wasn't quite as innocent as he imagined. She certainly hadn't cared about Liam's sister. And family was everything to him.

It was past time he accepted she wasn't the right woman for him.

Not by a long shot.

Chapter Fourteen

Harper ignored the sweat sliding down her back as she dropped her roller back into its pan before she stepped back a dozen steps to admire her handiwork. She'd painted the exterior a bright white and it was dazzling.

It was amazing what she'd achieved with a large quantity of paint that had been on sale and a lot of blood sweat and tears. She glanced at the extension ladders and scaffolding she'd hired. The company she'd hired them from would be here in the morning to take the scaffolding back.

Her giggle verged close to hysteria. She'd done it! She'd finished before she'd even imagined she would. And the white with dark gray trim had really brought the house back to life.

She sagged a little, her muscles sore and cramping a little. She'd clean all her brushes and rollers first, then she'd soak in a hot bubble bath. If she had the energy to move after that, she'd make a sandwich for dinner and collapse into bed.

Half-an-hour later she was soaking in the bath, half-heartedly scraping some of the paint off her hands. It'd been three weeks since she'd left Liam and not looked back. Three weeks where she'd worked herself into the ground trying to make her bed and breakfast a reality while squashing any thoughts of the man who'd taken up all the space in her heart.

No easy feat. Not when every quiet moment her thoughts returned to him.

She sighed heavily, a few bath bubbles separating and exploding. It was going to take her a long time to forget about him. She touched the shell she'd been wearing around her neck ever since she'd attached a cord to it. If it wasn't for her dreams and ambitions maybe they would have had a chance together, a real relationship.

Or maybe she'd saved herself a whole lot of heartache by leaving him before she'd fallen for him completely, only to have him walk away once the novelty had worn off for him.

She released the shell and closed her eyes before she slipped further under the bubbles. She might be hurting now but she would have been hurt a whole lot more if she'd stayed. Her instincts had been all wrong about him.

What if they weren't? What if you left the one man who might have made you happy?

Weariness slid over her, chasing away anymore doubts. She'd chosen her path, now she'd just have to live with it.

Suddenly she was camping with her dad, flames crackling in front of her as they pushed their long-handled camping sandwich makers into the coals. Her dad's brown eyes gleamed as he lifted his toaster free then pulled its handles apart to check his ham and cheese toasted sandwich. "This one is golden brown perfection." He looked at her. "What about yours?"

"I've got egg on mine and I don't want the yolk oozing."

Her dad laughed. "Looks like I'll be eating first then, munchkin."

"Dad, I'm thirteen! Hardly a munchkin anymore."

"You'll always be my munchkin, sweetheart."

She was suddenly eighteen then and standing arm-in-arm with her dad while admiring the crumbling estate they'd just bought together. Though the mansion was cosmetically ugly, the bones of it were solid, even the electrics and plumbing were good. Anything that had needed to be fixed over the years had just been left unattended.

"She's a beauty," her dad said, a note of satisfaction in his voice. "We're going make her shine again, munchkin."

She didn't bother correcting the nickname he used. Instead she giggled. "Then she's going to need a lot of spit and polish."

"She certainly will."

"And a lot of money, Dad. I'll see if I can get work in the city and—"

"Let's not go rushing into anything. I've still got a little bit of a nest egg we can live on while we bring this beauty back to its former glory."

"Dad, your nest egg is barely enough to cover groceries every week. We have a mortgage now and bills to pay, not to mention all the paint, curtains, flooring and everything else we'll have to buy. Then there's the fences."

"Whoa, munchkin. One thing at a time, hey? I suggest we start with the paddock on the right with that lovely big lake. Our neighbor has a tractor, I'll pay him to come and slash the weeds so the grass can grow, then we'll fence it into separate paddocks and start earning an income from some horses. We'll do the other paddocks once word gets out about our agistment here."

She nodded. "If we stay here we'll save money on rent."

"That's my girl. You can have the self-sufficient room downstairs. I'm happy to take one of the bedrooms upstairs."

"Are you sure?"

"Of course I'm sure, munchkin. You deserve the best." His eyes gleamed. "And I won't be around forever. I only hope that when I'm gone you'll find a man to fall head over heels in love with. A man who'll be your best friend and someone you can trust."

"Dad, stop talking like that...like you're leaving me soon." She shivered. "You're all I've got."

He nodded, his silver-gray hair like a beacon around his gaunt face even as his arm tightened around her. "I don't want you believing that a good, decent man would ever consider abandoning you. Not like your mother abandoned us."

She stiffened. Of course he was right, she knew that, but a part of her was cynical enough to wonder if a mother could leave her own child, what chance did she have of a man sticking around?

"I wish I could believe that," she said softly.

"I wish you did too, munchkin."

The next second she was looking down at her father in a hospital bed, his face chalky white and his eyes closed. He was fighting for his life, but she knew his fight was coming to an end. She kissed his forehead and whispered, "Dad, it's okay if you need to leave, I'm going to be all right." A tear slipped down her cheek as his heart monitor machine beeped loudly. "I'll always love you."

Chapter Fifteen

Liam drove slowly over the cattle grid and along the pot-holed, unsealed road, but there was nothing slow about his determination. He'd been a fool letting Harper slip through his fingers, and if he had to fight the sheikh to get her back he'd use everything in his arsenal to do just that.

The trees soon gave way to paddocks and he glanced out his side window, noting that the three horses in the paddock had grown to seven. He smiled. He was happy for her. She was on her way to financial success.

It wasn't until he topped the rise ahead that he pushed on the brake pedal and blinked at the house that no longer looked like wrack and ruin. It looked...incredible. It was as if he was staring at another house altogether.

He let out a whistle. The sheikh had been busy. Harper would be ecstatic and no doubt forever grateful to Korian. Liam clenched the steering wheel until his knuckles went white. He loosened his grip. He wasn't without his own wealth and resources. More importantly, his feelings were already invested.

Aside from money, he doubted the sheikh had anything more to show Harper other than lust.

He released the brake pedal and cruised forward, his every cell vibrating with an urgency to see her again. He wasn't giving her up without fight, not this time. Not ever again.

He'd been a hypocrite of the highest order to look at her as mercenary. He and his brothers had done everything imaginable to earn money while working hard and enduring all kinds of criticism as they brought their dreams into reality and became wealthy in their own right.

The dream she'd shared with her father meant she was also willing to make any sacrifice necessary to bring their dream into fruition.

He sighed heavily. His lack of trust had led him to believe she'd betrayed him. But the truth was he'd been ready to condemn her at the first opportunity just to save himself from future heartbreak. In matters of the heart, he was a slow learner. It'd taken him three weeks to figure out just how much Harper meant to him and how much his parents fake happiness and then their deaths had affected him.

He should have listened to Ned's sage advice when he'd questioned him giving up on her and that she deserved better than the sheikh.

He slowed his car to park next to Harper's white SUV. He only hoped Korian hadn't bought Harper's soul in her trying to fulfill her and her dad's dream.

He pressed his car's horn to make sure she was aware of him. After all this time she wouldn't be expecting him now. Though, no doubt, the sheikh was a regular visitor.

He pushed open his car door and slammed it shut behind him with more force than necessary. Korian had been a viper slithering between the cracks of Lim and Harper's budding relationship before they'd had time to blossom together.

Shaking off his dark thoughts, he adjusted his suit jacket before he strode toward the front door of her home. Though the ripped screen door was no longer in place, he was surprised to find the patchy old door had yet to be replaced.

Lifting his fisted hand, he rapped on the door. It creaked open and he paused before he stepped inside. "Harper?"

When there was no response, sudden ill-ease swept through him. Was she all right? Surely her front door would be locked if she was home? That her SUV had been parked outside told him she was more than likely here.

He stalked through the kitchen and headed down the short hallway that led to her self-sufficient living area. He only vaguely noted that no renovations had been done inside as he entered her domain. He turned away from her kitchenette and lounge and walked into her bedroom. Her bed with its mint green cover was empty and neatly made. He frowned. Was that steam coming out of her bathroom?

Opening its door, he froze as he took in his wildflower as she slept in the tub, her strawberry-blonde hair damp from the steam, the ends dark and saturated from the bathwater. Bubbles half-covered her, but not enough to stop his heart from jerking erratically, along with his dick.

Lord help him, he'd missed her so much.

The splotches of white paint on her hands and arms only made her more adorable. But it was the shell hanging from its cord around her neck that made him exhale sharply. She *did* still care about him.

She stirred, her eyes opening, then widening at seeing him. "Liam?" She sat up, water and bubbles sliding off her top half and exposing her breasts fully. "Wh-what are you doing here?"

"Your front door was open," he said in a guttural voice. "I was worried."

She snorted. "As you can see, I'm fine." She nodded at the towel on the towel rack. "Pass me that, would you?"

"Of course." He handed her the soft, lilac-colored towel before she stood, then stepped out onto the floor mat.

She dried herself slowly, her eyes darkening as she looked at him. "You didn't answer my question. What are you doing here—three weeks after I left you?"

He grimaced. "It took me that long to realize how wrong I'd been...about everything."

"Slow learner, huh?"

"It would seem so, at least when it comes to love."

"Love?" she repeated, her towel dropping from her hands as she looked up at him. "Do you actually believe such an emotion exists?"

"You loved your dad," he reminded. "You love this house and property, and the dream you had with you dad to make it a bed and breakfast."

She nodded, then said softly, "That's true."

"Though I've never been in love before I know I can't stop thinking about you and regretting ever letting you go without a fight." His stare dropped to her heavy breasts and the sharp points of her nipples, her flat stomach and the strip of blonde hair that highlighted her femininity.

"Would you like me to get dressed so you can concentrate?" she asked, a smile curling her lips.

"Yes. No." He shook his head. "My body can't lie. It still wants you badly."

She glanced down at his erection that bulged beneath his pants. "My body wants yours just as badly." She stepped toward him, lifting her arms then to hold onto his shoulders. "I need you," she said huskily.

Chapter Sixteen

Harper's heart skipped a beat as she waited for Liam's response.

His eyes flashed and he groaned, dropping his head so that his mouth claimed hers while his hands cupped her ass and he dragged her against him. She submitted to his lips that were soft and yet unyielding, taking everything she had to give and more.

Holy shit. She'd missed this. Missed him. The dream she'd had earlier only reinforced her need to believe in him. It'd been her insecurities that had made her doubt him...doubt them.

Her father had been right all along...it was time she learned to trust someone, and Liam was the one man she should have put her faith in from the start. That their chemistry was off the charts was just a bonus.

He toed off his shoes even as she thrust off his jacket and unbuttoned his shirt, revealing his powerful chest and golden expanse of skin. She broke their kiss to press her lips against his collarbone, then his thudding heart. It was beating like a jackhammer, his heightened needs matching hers.

Her chest suddenly tight, she crouched to kiss along the corded warmth of his stomach, loving the salty herbal scent of his skin, the rippling strength of his abs. Her hands trembled as she undid his zipper and button, then pulled them down along with his boxer briefs.

His cock reared up, powerful and long, and she clasped the base as she looked up at him, holding his stare as she opened her mouth to enclose the tip of him before slowly suctioning him almost to the base. She moaned a little, wishing she could work his cock all the way in.

He didn't seem mind.

"Harper," he groaned. His hands pushed through her hair, prickling her scalp until it burned. That it turned her on wasn't even a question. Everything Liam did made her wet.

She bobbed her head up and down, devouring as much of him as possible. She loved the taste of him, salty like the ocean, yet minty like the herbs growing in a forest.

She couldn't get enough.

"Enough," he growled, his voice raw as he spoke the one word that was in direct contrast to what she wanted—until he admitted, "I want to come inside you while I make you come."

She released him and he pulled her up and sealed his mouth to hers as he marched her backward into her bedroom. She fell onto her bed and he followed her down, his hard body contrary to the soft comforter beneath her spine.

He froze, his eyes holding hers. "I didn't bring a condom."

She shook her head. "It's all right. I'm on contraception now, and I'm clean."

His eyes flashed with something that looked like jealousy, maybe even resentment, then he shook his head. "I am too, clean I mean." He laughed, though it sounded pained. "I can't wait a second longer, wildflower."

She opened her legs and wrapped them around his hips. He one-handed his shaft and guided it to her entrance, his eyes burning into hers even as he thrust deep inside her with a satisfied grunt.

She inhaled sharply. Despite his size, his bared cock felt all kinds of perfect inside her. Then he began pumping with long, hard thrusts that quickly increased speed and intensity, the friction burning and heating her from the inside out, turning her into a volcano on the verge of eruption.

He bent and kissed her, and she surrendered to his mastery, counterthrusting against his rhythmic thrusts while their tongues danced and swayed and he conquered her once and for all. The cumulative heat ruptured inside and her heart exploded into a million pieces while every other piece of her shattered in rapturous bliss.

He followed her to nirvana, grinding into her one last time, his groan long and loud as his seed blasted inside her and their slick bodies clung together like he was just as afraid as she was that they'd lose each other again.

He stayed buried inside of her as he kissed her brow, one of his hands playing with the shell hanging from its cord around her neck. His gaze lifted and caught hers. "That was incredible."

She nodded, too stunned to put into words how damn good they were together.

He blinked, his piercing blue stare darkening. "But as much as I loved having sex with you, I didn't come here expecting it."

She managed a shaky smile. "I'm not complaining."

"I'm definitely not complaining either, wildflower. It's just...I have no willpower when it comes to you. You're all I think about."

"Then I'm glad I'm not alone." She blinked up at him. "You're all I think about, too."

"More even than your renovations?" he teased.

"Now that's pushing it," she said with a laugh. "Painting this house was the only thing stopping me from thinking about you all the damn time."

He reared his head back. "*You* painted the whole exterior?"

"I did." She shrugged. "I knew I had to start on something major that wouldn't entirely break my budget. So I decided the exterior walls were as good a place to start as anywhere."

"Korian didn't hire a team of painters for you?"

She narrowed her eyes at him, her stomach tightening a little as the truth slowly dawned. "Why would Korian do that?"

"You had a business plan with him."

"The same plan that had him mixing his business with pleasure?"

"I imagined so," he conceded. "Was I wrong?"

She pushed at his shoulders, all but forcing him to disconnect before she rolled to her side of the bed and sat with her back to him.

She looked at her floor, seeing every little bit of shabby threadbare carpet. "Did you really believe I'd fuck you while I was fucking someone else?"

She flinched as he reached out and touched her lower back. "I didn't have much time to think about anything once I arrived and saw you in the bath," he said gently. "Least of all Korian."

She understood now why Liam's eyes had flashed with envy and resentment when she said she was protected against pregnancy. He'd thought she'd been screwing the sheikh. She exhaled raggedly. Perhaps she would have thought the same thing too if she'd been in his shoes.

"I didn't accept either one of his offers," she said quietly. "I couldn't, not knowing that he'd own a piece of my soul if I did."

"You did the right thing." He drew her around to face him. "You have no idea how happy that makes me. I thought I'd lost you to him. I came here prepared to fight dirty if needed so I could win you back from him."

She looked up at him, his blond hair shining like a halo. Her heart melted. "What are you trying to say?"

He reached out and drew her closer. His eyes held hers. "What I'm trying to say wildflower is that I can't stop thinking about you." His stare softened. "I love you."

"You do?" she asked, her pulse thudding in her ears while adrenaline and hopeless need poured through her. For a second doubt and mistrust reared it's ugly head, but she pushed it back. Her dad had been right all along. Just because her mother had left, it didn't mean a good, decent man would abandon her. And Liam *was* a good man through and through.

"I love you too," she said huskily. She touched the shell at her throat. "I don't know how we'll make this work, but I want to be with you."

He cupped her face and pressed his lips against hers. "I promise you we *will* make it work. It's not even an hour's drive to here."

"You'll come here every night?"

"Just try and keep me away." He grinned. "And it just so happens I love renovating. We'll do it together...if you'll have me."

She laughed then. "Just try and keep away from me! You're stuck here with me now. Except for those days and nights I hang out with you at your penthouse."

"You'd do that?"

"A few days a week at your place would be a lovely break."

"It's the perfect solution," he agreed huskily. Then he leaned forward and covered her mouth with his, and any residual fears and worries faded to nothing as she leaned into him and accepted him with everything she had.

Epilogue

Four months later...

Harper climbed out of Liam's Range Rover where he'd stopped it on the rise of the property. Behind them, seventeen horses grazed on the grass, with brand new shelters tucked into the corner of each paddock.

On the other side of the road, new railed fencing showcased paddocks cleared of weeds, the new grass thick, green and inviting, and ready for more horses to graze it. Going by all the enquiries it wouldn't take long to fill the large paddocks that allowed for a handful of horses, along with the smaller paddocks designed for one or two horses.

Liam stepped behind her, his arms settling around her before she leaned against him. "How does it feel seeing your dreams come true?" he asked tenderly.

"Surreal," she admitted, drinking in the sight before she turned in his arms and drank in an even better one. "I couldn't have done it without you."

"I sped up the process, that's all," he said. Pride laced his voice. "Given time, I have no doubt you would have done all this on your own."

He turned then, keeping an arm around her waist as they took in the view of the house. It shone white under the sunlight, the now graveled road and green leafy trees highlighting its majesty. Then there was the organic garden at the back, which she planned to use to help feed the guests.

Liam had convinced her to hire a cook and a cleaner, both of whom would start next week when her first B&B guests arrived. The interior of the house was a masterpiece, one she was sure her guests would appreciate. That she and Liam still had their own personal living space, which they'd also renovated, meant they had all the privacy they loved when they didn't feel a need to mingle with others.

"We should probably stop gawping and get some food and drinks ready before your family arrives," she suggested.

"We probably should," he agreed, kissing her scalp before releasing her. "My sister, brothers and their wives, along with their children, will be a good test for us."

She sighed happily. "I'm sure they'll love it here as much as we do."

That she planned on using horses for therapy in the future was just another dream she knew would come to fruition sooner rather than later. She also hoped to keep some of her property free for those neglected horses that needed rest and rehabilitation before rehoming them.

"I doubt anyone could love this place more than us," he declared.

"Or my dad," she said thickly.

"I'm sure he's smiling down at us right now," Liam said gently, "as proud of you as I am."

She followed him to the car then, and as Liam drove them to the house, she was aware of how very lucky she and Liam had been finding one another. Their future shone with as much promise as the restored, majestic house that shone in front of them.

Want even more contemporary stories by Mel Teshco?
Look out for Sons of the Sheikh! A brand new series coming soon in 2024!

Scorpion

His sting is as lethal as his charm

Sheikh Aziz Hadi might be a player who knows how to charm the panties off women, but that means very little when the one woman he wants—Zamira Fasih—is also the one woman he can't have. She's the daughter of a sheikh from a neighboring country bordering his province. That they're at war means there is no way he can talk to her, let alone date her. Then he sees her at the markets and he can't deny the impulse to take what—who—he wants.

Zamira Fasih is not interested in Aziz, at least that's what she tells herself. He and his family sided with an enemy of her father's and now her people are paying the ultimate price. The Hadi family are scum, and Aziz is the worst of them. He's not worthy of her attention, if only she'd stop damn well thinking about him! Then he kidnaps her and expects her to like him—he'd better think again!

She is promised to another man who will help end the war and the death of her people, and nothing will change her mind. Not even the famous scorpion charm Aziz is renowned for.

In the meantime...check out the first book in my new mafia series, Wedlocked.

Chapter One of Wedlocked

Sabrina

The euphoria slipping over me like a second skin was nothing short of liberating as I sashayed my way through throngs of glittering guests, surreptitiously eavesdropping on their conversations while I sipped on overpriced bubbles.

I was born for this subterfuge...for the thrill of the hunt. Except, I was no hunter, I wasn't even a spy. Hell, I wasn't even meant to be here tonight.

I was Sabrina Costa, the one and only daughter of the Costa mafia family. Not only was I invaluable, a pawn to my family, I'd become somewhat invisible, too. I could put up with being a pawn—weren't we all?—but it grated my gears that I'd never been allowed to bask in the power and prestige given freely to my brother, Salvatore.

I was determined that would change tonight and I'd be the one who'd uncover what was really going down with our rival mobster family, the Agostinos.

A shiver of unease threatened to take away my swagger. If my father or my brother caught me here at our rival's house, I'd never be without a guard again. Hell, there was a chance I mightn't even make it out of this party alive, if my own family didn't kill me first.

The knowledge sent my pulse racing, my breath catching in the throat. A smile curled my lips. Damn, it was good to finally feel alive! Being groomed to be the next bride to some Frankenstein mobster wasn't my one and only objective in life. That was pretty much last on my bucket list.

I was determined to prove one way or another that I wasn't just a pretty face. I had power too, along with connections, they were just more...subtle. I touched my plump, lower lip. One didn't need to fire a semi-automatic when poisoned lipstick could do the job with so much more...finesse.

Not that I was planning on killing anyone tonight. Information was all I desired. After all, information was power and I craved that rush like nothing else, craved to experience what my brother did on a daily basis.

Being a woman hadn't curbed my killer instincts, if anything it'd honed them sharper. I wasn't a behind-the-scenes type of woman, I never had been. I might have been homeschooled and kept socially inept, but it hadn't dulled my brain. My teachers had quickly learned I was bright. Too bright at times for the social role I'd one day soon be forced to play—an arranged marriage to propel my mafia family's standing to the top of the heap once and for all.

I had a fair idea now which man out of the three other mobster families my father planned to assign me to, and it most certainly wouldn't be one of the Agostino brothers. My dad was already leaning toward the Accardi family underboss, anything to push back the powerful Agostino uprising.

I'd be fed to the wolves, quite literally, my virtue of no importance once my father agreed upon my worth. That I was a beauty along with being an innocent would no doubt increase my potential groom-to-be's desire to have me...to own me. And probably hurt me. It would be considered a small price to pay so that my family could wrestle back mobster dominance.

Little wonder I'd been guarded so stringently. My role as daughter had been just as important, possibly more so, than the role of my brother. It meant I'd had few friends or social interactions growing up and I'd had to strive to be adept in a crowd, playing it cool when inwardly my ego and passionate nature battled with my fragile insecurities and inexperience with social engagements.

The one benefit from my upbringing was that no one recognized me now. I was a stranger here, slipping through the party like a wraith in my wraparound, red sheaf dress and silver heels. I'd ensured my striking platinum blonde hair, a trait I shared with Salvatore, was pulled off my face in a braided topknot. I hadn't had time to do much of anything else. Even my lipstick had been applied hastily in the back of the cab I'd ordered to pick me up a block away from my family home.

The Agostinos lived an hour west of New York City, their house overlooking the same Promenade River that my family's house did. Except us Costas lived an hour east of New York. It didn't stop the turf rivalry between us. It was legendary and spanned generations thanks to our forebears who'd moved from Sicily with nothing but a gun, and whole lot of grit and determination.

"I hear Ethan won't be joining us for at least another hour."

My ears pricked at the name of the Agostino underboss, and I tuned into the gossip ensuing between the three young, designer clad women dripping with jewels and barely withheld envy.

"He's celebrating privately first, if you get my drift," said a brunette, her sparkly diamond clips holding back the sides of her dead-straight hair.

Celebrating what, exactly? A pity I couldn't approach and straight out ask them. Not without drawing attention to myself.

"Surely there are enough girls willing to do him for free?" a dark-haired women asked, her hands fluttering as she fanned her flushed face. "Lord knows I'd do him in a heartbeat."

"Who says he wants them willing?" the brunette asked with a husky, evocative laugh. "Besides, you'd do anyone for free," she added with a malicious sniff.

I didn't hang around to hear the rest of their mean dialogue, instead I found myself drifting around the huge marble staircase while my thoughts also drifted. I only hoped my platinum wig, which I'd left lying on top of my pillow on my bed back home, would trick anyone who might look in on me until I returned home.

It'd be unlikely anyone would bother. It wasn't like I had a mother anymore to care about me and my father most certainly didn't. As for my brother, our bond was seriously close but even he was too busy lately in his role as our father's underboss to focus on me.

No one would miss me until morning.

In the meantime I had to be careful not to engage in conversation with anyone while being mindful my distinctive hair stayed pulled back so that I didn't stand out. Another frisson of excitement sparked through me as I edged through the crowd. I was just another beautiful face amongst these wealthy and overdressed guests.

The fact I might be one of the few women here without a clutch purse or cellphone was probably more noticeable than my hair. It'd been worth it though just so that I had no identification on me, no proof to get me caught out.

This is stupid! Reckless. Dangerous.

"And I wouldn't change a thing," I murmured to myself as I rounded the grand staircase with its glittering chandelier hanging high above.

I stopped as I inadvertently stumbled upon a discreet service entry elevator, where a harried young waiter pushed a cart of liquor and other supplies inside, the doors then sliding shut behind him.

My belly fluttered and my womb clenched. Was that where I'd find the underboss? Ethan might not yet be the don, but it would only be a matter of time before he took over from his father.

I shuddered. Ethan's father, Lorenzo, made my own dad look like Prince Charming. Violence might be a way of life for our families, but Lorenzo was as soulless as a man could get without already being in hell.

Even I'd heard rumors about the Agostino don's proclivities. He enjoyed inflicting pain and punishment, and got off on watching others suffer. Not even his family was safe. I could only imagine the sadistic children he'd raised.

The elevator doors reopened and a suited man stepped out. His dark eyes trawling over my silver-blonde hair, he asked, "You're here for Ethan?"

I blinked, then automatically nodded as realization kicked in. The soldier presumed I'd been hired to have sex with his boss. I ran an absent hand along the silky fabric of my short, fitted gown. I hadn't intended to dress like one of Ethan's whores, but who was I to deny fate? I wanted answers, what better way to get them than straight from the horse's mouth.

The suited man's eyes glinted. "I can see now why he has a thing for blondes. That lucky bastard really is celebrating tonight."

I managed a coy smile. Fuck. Did high-priced whores act cheap or did they swan around like celebrities? The whores that my dad and brother had brought into our home hadn't exactly been subtle about their intentions. But surely discretion was what a higher-end escort provided?

I sashayed past suited-man and stepped alone into the elevator, my panties already a little damp just thinking about what could happen upstairs with Ethan if I wasn't careful. He'd be expecting pre-celebration sex, probably hardcore stuff only the most experienced of women would know how to enjoy.

I swallowed as the doors slid shut and the elevator swept me upstairs. I'd seen pictures of Ethan. He might have been good looking if not for his hard eyes and the jagged white scar spreading halfway along his jaw. If his full lower lip hinted at sexuality, the thin upper lip hinted at cruelty.

He was something of a paradox to me even before the elevator doors slid open and I was greeted with the man himself...in all his naked glory.

If you'd like to know when my next book is available, as well as other pre-orders, cover reveals and other news, sign up for my newsletter: https://madmimi.com/signups/121695/join

Check out my website – http://www.melteshco.com/

You can also friend me on Facebook at https://www.facebook.com/mel.teshco

Or my author Facebook page at https://www.facebook.com/MelTeshcoAuthor

Contact me: melteshco@yahoo.com.au

If you enjoy my books I'd be delighted if you would consider leaving a review. This will help other readers find my books ☺

About the Author

I'm an award winning author who loves to write scorching hot contemporary and science fiction romance—stories I love to read. I love working from home, where my office window looks out over our 'block' of fourteen acres with gorgeous mountain views. After enjoying a stint as a foster carer for cats, I now have seven felines to entertain me, along with two dogs and two horses. But only when I'm not distracted by my three gorgeous daughters, one of whom—a teenager *shriek*—is still living at home. As for my husband...he's still waiting for retirement.

Want more Mel Teshco books?

Contemporary

Desert Kings Alliance

The Sheikh's Runaway Bride (book 1)

The Sheikh's Captive Lover (book 2)

The Sheikh's Forbidden Wife (book 3)

The Sheikh's Secret Mistress (book 4)

The Sheikh's Defiant Princess (book 5)

The Sheikh's Fake Fiancée (book 6)

The Sheikh's Royal Widow (book 7)

The Sheikh's Temporary Girlfriend (book 8)

Desert Kings Alliance Box Set (Volumes 1-4)

Desert Kings Alliance Box Set (Volumes 5-8)

Gangsters at War

Wedlocked (book 1)

Avenged (book 2)

Enforced (book 3)

Contracted (book4)

more coming soon...

Bachelor Brothers of Sydney

Highest Bid (book 1)

Bought at Auction (book 2)

Winning Offer (book 3)

The VIP Desire Agency

Lady in Red (book 1)

High Class (book 2)

Exclusive (book 3)

Liberated (book 4)

Uninhibited (book 5)

The VIP Desire Agency Boxed Set (all 5 books in the series)

Box sets with authors Christina Phillips & Cathleen Ross

Sheikhs & Billionaires

Taken by the Sheikh
Taken by the Billionaire
Taken by the Desert Sheikh
Resisting the Firefighter
Standalone longer length titles: (50k-100k)
As I Am
Standalone novellas and short stories: (15k-40K)
Her Dark Guardian
Stripped
Clarissa
Camilla
Selena's Bodyguard (also part of the Christmas Assortment Box)
Anthologies
Down and Dusty: The Complete Collection
The Christmas Assortment Box
Science Fiction
The Virgin Hunt Games
The Virgin Hunt Games volume 1
The Virgin Hunt Games volume 2
The Virgin Hunt Games volume 3
The Virgin Hunt Games volume 4
The Virgin Hunt Games volume 5
The Virgin Hunt Games volume 6
Alien Fugitives
Nero (book 1)
Jasper (book 2)
Sienna (book 3)
Damaris (book 4)
Dragons of Riddich
Kadin (prequel - book 1)
Asher (book 2)
Baron (book 3)

Dahlia (book 4)
Wyatt (book 5)
Valor (book 6)
The Queen (book 7)
Alien Hunger
Galactic Burn (book 1)
Galactic Inferno (book 2)
Galactic Flame (book 3)
Coming soon
Galactic Blaze (book 4)
Nightmix
Lusting the Enemy (book 1)
Abducting the Princess (book 2)
Seducing the Huntress (book 3)
Winged & Dangerous
Stone Cold Lover (book 1)
Ice Cold Lover (book 2)
Red Hot Lover (book 3)
Winged & Dangerous Box Set (all 3 books in the series)
Dirty Sexy Space continuity with Denise Rossetti
Yours to Uncover (book 1)
Mine to Serve (book 6)
Ours to Share (book 8)
Awakenings series with Kylie Sheaffe
No Ordinary Gift (book 1)
Believe (book 2)
Homecoming (book 3)
Standalone longer length titles: (50k-100k)
Dimensional
Mutant Unveiled
Shadow Hunter
Existence

Standalone novellas and short stories: (15k-40K)
Identity Shift
Moon Thrall
Blood Chance
Carnal Moon

Milton Keynes UK
Ingram Content Group UK Ltd.
UKHW010733220224
438165UK00001B/37